RITUALS
OF
SPRING

Rituals of Spring

Edited by Drea Talley

RITUALS OF SPRING
First Edition.
April 22, 2025

Periapt Press
PO Box 25693
Colorado Springs, CO 80936
www.periaptpress.com

ISBN: 979-8-9903639-6-0

For everyone who feels a weight lift when they see that first crocus blossom pushing up through the snow.

CONTENTS

PAINTING THE SEASONS

Nikki Flynn

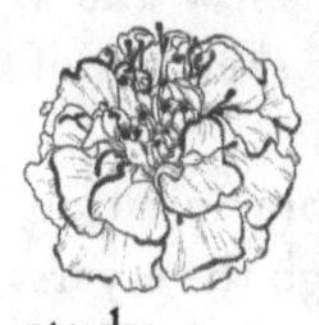 Naslyn clenched her jaw and failed to quash the tears welling up in her mind and body. Her nose tingled and she scrunched up her face while her stunned gaze immortalized the horrendous scene strewn about the study.

Sidhe, Merlin's staff, had crashed to the floor and splintered against the white stone. The effects of the last spell Merlin had cast leaked from its knob, green, blue, purple and red liquid oozing together. His fall threw books, inkpots, quills, and parchment from the desk, scattering everything to the floor. Merlin was normally tidy with everything arranged in its purposefully chosen place unless it was in use. He had a cumbersome oak desk, room for writing and reading. He only housed reference materials on magic and prophecies in his office so there was only a single tall and wide bookcase on a single wall. The fireplace behind the desk was dark with a fire having died out hours before when Merlin was expecting to work through the cold winter night.

The apprentice mage traipsed further into the room, towards where Merlin himself lay. One ginger step after another until she loomed over the staff. Her tears streamed down her face despite her best attempt at keeping her expression neutral. She failed to hide the grief that was still forming a knot in her chest. Naslyn recovered the staff then knelt beside her mentor. He was a petite man, young-looking despite his eons of existence. His soft-featured, oval face was bloodied from a head wound. Naslyn placed her hand on Merlin's forehead. His skin had cooled. His eyes were pale. She examined the wound at his temple. It had bled profusely into his long golden hair. Naslyn glanced at the desk and the dribbling red that had pooled after he fell. Shaking from being forced to confront Merlin's death, she pushed herself upright. Gritting her teeth she broke into sobs. There never would be enough tears to express the enormity of loss yet she cried oceans for her father figure and mentor. She mourned for herself and the work left undone. She tenderly brushed a hand down Merlin's face, closing his eyes.

The spell was still active in the staff, and so her grief would have to wait. Dutifully picking up where Merlin left off, Naslyn pulled on her thick, fur-lined poncho, then her snow boots. The dark-haired apprentice stepped into a sketch-like drawing that still sat on Merlin's desk. A sketch of a world white with snow and a lack of color against the rough pencil lines of the tree sketches of the forest.

Puffs of snow spewed out of the clouds. The precipitation layered blankets of white while Naslyn waddled through the layers of snow crunching beneath her boots. Around her, cloaked in the stillness and stabbing bright whiteness, hares fled from foxes while seals, bears, and caribou traversed the treacherous terrain. A faint shade of blue settled onto her skin, leaving her extremities too cold to easily soothe away. Naslyn fought the bursts of stabbing winds that fought to keep winter in place, reining over the world. Her fingers dug into Sidhe. Nothing was going to keep her from completing the task at hand. It had been her mentor's job before nature reclaimed him, and now she wore that mantle, carrying on the change of seasons and the passage of time that rested in the domain of magicians.

A burst of snow and air hit her forcefully, pushing her hood back. Naslyn turned away from the gust. She walked backward the final few paces to the first point she sought. Beneath the gnarled, bare towering ring of trees, Naslyn tapped the butt of Sidhe on the ground. A burst of green light cut through the icy winds, negating their biting power. She tapped the staff again, and the defanged gusts slowed to a soothing zephyr. In the area immediately around the staff, snow disintegrated revealing the brown and yellow grass that hibernated during the colder months. Naslyn repeated the spell, the coloration of the winter wilds, and green poured from Sidhe into the grass. The glowing peridot aura from the staff faded, then vanished.

Naslyn stamped through the weakened, softer snow, crossing from the ring of trees toward her next point for the spell. Among the worst parts of sorcery were the spells that required specific locations to work. Dread slowed her even as Sidhe dutifully warmed her hands and kept her energized. She hated knowing what was coming from her time shadowing Merlin. She was about to get wet in the middle of winter.

The task at hand was tedious, but if she stopped, the spell would likely need cast again. Magical effects wore off, subject to the fetters of time like everything else. Naslyn's boots crunched the remaining snow with each step toward the lake. The water needed to be thawed, color needed restored. It was no longer the age of white and grey. The chill that lingered for winter to let the flora of the world sleep needed dispelled.

Naslyn's breath was visible. Each huff out was relief, but each inhale was several jabbing daggers in her nose and mouth. Her airway was practically encrusted with frost as she approached the lake. Sidhe gained ten pounds during her journey between the first and second nexus for the season changing spell. With a shuddering groan and her teeth chattering preemptively, the apprentice tapped the staff on the ground beside the shore. A burst of warm light followed. Yellow then white pulsed through the ice and called the birds home from their distant migrations.

The caster breached the water, though the air still bared winter's fangs. Painful as it was, she picked up Merlin's mantle. She could already imagine her feet turning blue. Terror of frostbite and succumbing to the elements and exhaustion jolted her into action. Naslyn cast the spell again, radiating color from Sidhe. Her skin prickled and her limbs trembled. Winter stubbornly clung to the world despite her repeated attempts to excise its hold on the environment. She waved the wand and more ice melted. From beneath the melting snow lotuses and lily pads were revealed on the calm lake surface. Another sweeping gesture, then another splashed color onto the flowers and leaves. The greyscale was giving way to the vivacious world beneath the gloom. For good measure Naslyn rapped the staff several times on the lakebed. She jumped when movement caught her eye. She laughed off her foolery upon recognizing the fish swimming about freely as they did when Merlin brought warmth to the world.

Proud of her progress and now unconcerned with the chill that had settled into her bones, Naslyn waded to shore. The world wasn't restored yet, but she was close. The spell had one more nexus where she needed to cast away the snow and let the sunshine and rain rule over the sprouting seeds. She took a moment to wring the water from her robes and empty the water from her boots. If she had thought ahead she would have doffed them before she channeled the spell in the lake. The apprentice pushed the thought aside then stepped into her shoes to pick up her journey.

The first stretch of her walk made her think Jack Frost had given up his crown and abdicated to Verna Rains, but a blinding gust cut into her damp flesh and robes after she stepped foot onto the trail to the nexus. Naslyn's dark hair scattered and she blocked her face using her forearm and her outer robes. Imitating a vampire hiding from the sun, Naslyn's steps continued while a constant wind barked at her. The snow and ice on the trail had started shrinking away, but that had given way to other treacherous conditions. She slipped in mud and hit the ground. She groaned and remained still while pain radiated through her elbow which had collided with a stone. The wind stopped briefly. Naslyn recovered Sidhe, then after she advanced up the hillside trail several paces, the gale-force once more tried to expel her from the magical painting. Naslyn dug in, determined to complete Merlin's work. Her eyes, squinted from the wind and debris, drifted to the staff her mentor carried and settled on the crack where the colors had leaked from the staff's knob. It was in that moment as she breached the clouds that Naslyn knew what had happened to Merlin. Jack Frost in all of his stubbornness had succeeded in unsummoning Merlin from the painted world where the seasons were changed and time carried on into eternity. Old Man Winter, the bitter, harsh king, refused to relinquish control of the world, and that selfishness had left her an orphan.

Exhaustion and doubt had weighed her down more than wet clothes or Sidhe's cumbersome shape and size. Now heat from her anger fueled her and she exhaled the darkness that kept her in the shadow of Merlin in her mind. In the white and grey fog of the mountain peak, she was excited to usher in spring. The whipping, shrill gusts continued around her, but their coldness no longer affected her. Naslyn warmed herself with anger boiling her blood. The swirling cold and threats of snow were balked by her stabbing the staff into the ground. Naslyn repeated the defiant action, the last leg of the spell. Visibility returned to the mountain and clouds broke apart.

The apprentice stopped the spell only when she could see the sky clearly. She brandished Sidhe and with a flick of her wrist, the staff painted the melancholy grey skies that promised snow into a bright blue. More paint followed. Trees were hit with tiny speckles of green, then buds appeared, ready to grow into shady fruit bearing titans. The first birds settled, summoned from the second use of the spell. The sun's pale white shade was darkened to a vibrant yellow, and the more paint was spattered the more she waved the staff around. Snow and ice vanished. The brown and yellow grass became pale green, ready to darken with the first rain. The blizzard gales turned to a relaxing zephyr carrying seeds and spores to their new homes. Early blooming flowers promised rainbows and warm days with fluffy clouds, occasional showers, then the turn of the seasons to scorching summer.

Naslyn took Sidhe and staggered away from the edge of the cliff. She found a grey tree in a light sleep, nearly ready to wake and start its morning. Beneath its might she found comfort in having done what Merlin had intended. Her heart was heavy with grief and it always would be, but she was the one who now oversaw the seasons. With the task done and nothing of immediate importance keeping her stoic, Naslyn's tears cascaded to the world below. Her sobs watered the growing saplings and washed away the last of winter's presence. Before she was done, each droplet gathered in a gorge and flowed, carrying silt and her hopes for the future to a far away place and time.

F!RE BY MOONLIGHT

S.R. Paradigm

Princess Thessalyn of East Rodanthia was finally getting married.

At least, the king and queen *hoped* she would be getting married. No one had actually informed the princess of her impending nuptials.

Yet.

"What did you say the new herald's name was? Badger? Ermine? Wolverine?" the princess asked her lady's maid, trying to distract herself from the elaborate style the girl was painstakingly creating with her hair. She'd not met the new herald yet but expected him to be escorting her today.

Thessalyn kept her hair long, as was the custom for those of a certain status in East Rodanthia, but she preferred the simpler braids and twists Liana typically plaited for her. Today's style involved the maid twisting seemingly infinite curls into her auburn hair and pinning them up with bejeweled clips and combs.

"Badgeford, Your Highness."

"Yes. Of course." Thessalyn glowered at her reflection. "Isn't this all a bit much, Liana? It seems you've pinned half the treasury to my head."

Liana smiled, "Your mother insisted, Your Highness, something about important visitors from the west."

"From the west? Hm. I wonder if Father's treaty with our prickly neighbors is finally completed."

About twenty minutes later, or at *least* four hours if one were to ask Thessalyn, Liana deemed the princess appropriately adorned for court. The maid helped Thessalyn to her feet and stepped around her, adjusting a curl here, a dress pleat there until she was satisfied that everything was as it should be. The princess stared at her visage in the looking glass and felt there was rather more dress than woman. Four layers of sheer silver silk underskirts clung to the princess' legs which were further adorned in deep green tights, which were just barely visible through the layers. Her chemise of the same silver silk draped decoratively across her bust and down her arms, gathering above the elbows and flowing dramatically toward the floor. The heavily boned bodice, a deep green velvet that brightened the princess' grey-green eyes, cinched her waist above a matching open overskirt.

The princess turned back and forth slowly, observing the leafy silver embroidery that adorned the overskirt and bodice, and sighed dramatically, "I look like a topiary—a gilded topiary."

Liana tsked and corrected the princess with laughter in her eyes, "Gilding is done with gold, not silver, Your Highness."

"A *silver*-gilded topiary, then." The princess grumbled half-heartedly.

"The most beautiful of topiaries, I am sure, Your Highness," the maid replied seriously, "Well pruned and finely decorated."

Thessalyn finally laughed, "Indeed. You have outdone yourself, Liana, thank you. Well, I guess we're ready."

Just in time, it seemed, as moments later, a crisp knock announced that the new herald had arrived to escort her to the event.

"Your Highness?" the new herald inquired politely, "His Majesty requests your prompt appearance at court this afternoon."

"Yes, yes. I'm coming." Thessalyn sighed, gathered the borderline unreasonable number of skirts, and headed toward the corridor.

The herald bowed and gestured for the princess to precede him toward the great hall.

As they made their way, the princess smirked to herself and asked, "*Badger*, isn't it? Are you enjoying your new post as herald?"

"I, er, yes, Your Highness." The herald's voice dipped nervously as he responded, "It is a fine position; I am quite honored."

Thessalyn stopped and spun on her heel, causing the young man to trip and nearly run into her. "Don't do that," she said quietly, but firmly, catching and holding the herald's eyes.

"Apologies. I—Your Highness?"

"Don't agree with me when I'm clearly wrong," the princess sighed, "I know for a fact that your name is Badgeford. You should have corrected me."

"C-*correct* you?" the young man stuttered, clearly horrified at the mere idea of such a thing, "I couldn't possibly..." his voice trailed off as the princess began to glower at him.

"You can. And you will." Thessalyn stated, poking a finger into the man's chest, "Or you won't be my herald very long. You understand your role, don't you? My herald doesn't just escort me to appointments or announce me, he is my eyes and ears in this castle and the kingdom itself." She waved an arm around them.

Badgeford nodded vigorously, his grey eyes wide, but attentive.

"If I am to serve my people, I must know the *truth* of things, not the sanitized, embellished version that the nobles and would-be-nobles spout off in hopes of gaining Our favor. And that includes knowing when I am wrong. An accident of birth does not make one infallible, Badgeford, and I must insist that you remember that."

"I—yes, Your Highness," the herald bowed deeply, but began to relax, "I will remember."

"Excellent." Thessalyn grinned and turned back toward their destination, "Now, let's try again, shall we? *Badger*, isn't it? Are you enjoying your new post as herald?"

The herald smiled broadly, adjusted his livery, and hurried after the young woman who would someday be his queen, "Pardon, Your Highness, but the name's Badge*ford*, and I expect that I shall enjoy my post very much."

The midday sun shone in through the arched windows of the corridor, tinting the grey stone with warm gold tones and casting shadows beneath the heavy tapestries that adorned the walls. It was just as well that the space was well lit, as Thessalyn had a habit of jogging down the hall at a quite un-princess-like pace when no witnesses were about.

As they arrived at the ancient, heavy doors of the hall, a pair of guards in full, formal dress greeted them with a salute and exchanged knowing glances as the princess caught her breath and adjusted her skirts. Only when she had signaled her readiness did they turn and open the walnut doors.

Badgeford took a deep breath, aimed a split-second grin at the princess, and stepped into the cavernous room. After a heartbeat of a pause, he announced, with no hint of his earlier nervousness, "Her Royal Highness, Princess Thessalyn, Jewel of the East, Heir to the great kingdom of East Rodanthia."

The herald stepped quickly aside and bowed deeply as Thessalyn glided into the room. "Floated" was the term that her etiquette instructors had used, but she always felt the movement was more like ice skating at an exceptionally slow pace.

The Hall was overflowing with people.

Nobles, merchants, and every foreign dignitary who was currently in residence were in attendance. In fact, it even seemed that most of the household staff had managed to squeeze themselves into the room.

It was at this point that the princess began to wonder whether she was missing an important detail or two about what was happening today.

Having at least been briefed that this was a more formal occasion, Thessalyn smiled at the crowd and approached the dais where her parents sat. She curtsied deeply, but raised an eyebrow pointedly as she rose, seeking some hint from her parents as to the situation.

Her mother refused to make eye contact with her.

Her father, however, grinned broadly and waved for her to come join them, "Ah, my Jewel, you are, as ever, an absolute vision."

Thessalyn scowled at the king as she made her way up the stairs and took a seat next to her father. "Father," she whispered through a demure smile, "what's going on? And since when am I the 'Jewel of the East'?"

Her father just smiled and patted her hand gently before standing to address the crowd. "Thank you for joining us here today to celebrate the most wonderful of news. After two and a half years of negotiations, we have finally reached agreement with our neighbors to the west. Please join me in welcoming, from West Rodanthia, our new allies!"

The crowd erupted in cheers and applause. Thessalyn clapped politely and watched curiously as two men stepped forward from the crowd. An odd pair, for while they were clearly the West Rodanthian delegation, they appeared to have nothing else in common, neither appearance, style, nor demeanor.

The taller man, and tall he was, stood over a full head above his companion. If Thessalyn was spring blooming out of winter, this man was summer—blazing into autumn. His summery complexion and nearly black hair were both several shades darker than was common here; most East Rodanthians shared Thessalyn's own paler, creamy skin and lighter hair in blondes and browns. He wore a long, dark cloak which displayed the distinctive sharp lines and bold colors of the west but completely concealed his clothing. What really caught the princess' attention, however, was the man's expression, which she thought more at home on a cat who'd gotten lost in the creamery.

The shorter man, clearly a herald by his dress, was much lighter in his coloring. With much paler skin and hair that was nearly blonde, it seemed that the two men hailed from different ends of the continent rather than the same country. Were it not for the distinctive styling of his dress, he could have easily been mistaken for a local here in the east.

The herald looked miserable. This did not, however, impede his addressing the crowd.

"Your Grace," the herald began, "you honor us with such a fine welcome. On behalf of all West Rodanthia, we are pleased to finalize the treaty with your country today. To that end, it is my great pleasure to present His Royal Highness, Prince Floriant, Knight of the Seventh Order, Keeper of the Sacred Flame, and..." the herald paused looking, somehow, even more miserable.

The taller man elbowed him in the ribs.

The herald grimaced and continued in a strained voice, "and five-time winner of the Annual West Rodanthian Quilting Competition." The herald bowed deeply and stepped aside.

The attendees looked at each other, confused, and then began to clap awkwardly.

The taller man grinned widely and addressed the king, "Your Grace," then turned to Thessalyn, "Your Highness, I am most pleased to deliver the final outstanding clause of our alliance," he paused, caught Thessalyn's eyes, and then spun in a circle, dropping his cloak dramatically, and announced, "your treaty bride!"

The room fell silent.

The audience stared.

The queen gasped, horrified.

Thessalyn's jaw dropped.

The king laughed heartily, slapping his knee. He sat back down beside his daughter and said, "Ah, Prince Floriant, your father did warn me of your odd sense of humor."

Beneath the now abandoned cloak, the prince was clothed in a single shining white garment. The floor-length silk *wedding* gown, for it could surely be described no differently, flowed elegantly as the prince completed his turn, facing the king again. The bright fabric shone in contrast to the man's bronze complexion and thick, dark hair. Iridescent embroidery shimmered gently as the cloth settled about the man's strong legs, the thin material clinging to muscled thighs and dancing around his calves. The delicate fabric draped precariously low across the prince's chest, displaying the strength of his shoulders.

Floriant curtsied, graceful as any lady of a noble house, the smooth silk threatening to split beneath the muscles of his arms, flexing as he lifted the skirt delicately. He turned to Thessalyn with a cheerful smile, "I hope I meet your expectations, my lady?"

Recovering her jaw from the floor, the princess summoned a court-appropriate smile and leaned over to her father, her eyes still taking in the man before her, "I take it I'm to be the *groom*, then?"

Her father chuckled softly and nodded, "Indeed my dear, indeed."

"And, ah, when is this wedding supposed to be happening?"

Her mother gasped, "Why, never, if I—"

The king raised a hand, and the queen paused unhappily, "Next month, on the full moon."

"Right." Thessalyn whispered, noticing how the gown left very little of her betrothed's muscular frame to the imagination, "Could we have it sooner?"

The queen gasped again, but the king laughed and raised his voice, "My Jewel, don't leave the poor boy waiting, why don't you take your... bride, was it? to the gardens to become better acquainted?"

"It would be my pleasure." Thessalyn rose, stepped down from the dais, and curtsied to her parents, "by your leave."

The king waved them away and smiled warmly as his daughter offered the tall man her arm. He laid his fingers gently upon the offered arm, allowing himself to be led out of the Hall, his skirt flouncing gently beside hers.

"How can you let our only daughter marry that... that—" the queen hissed at him under her breath, a smile still plastered across her features.

"Prince?" he whispered back as the crowd began to chatter, "Didn't you hear her? She *agreed* to marry him! She's turned down every eligible man in four kingdoms."

His wife's tone softened as she absorbed what he'd said, "Oh. Oh, yes, dear, you're quite right; she did *somehow* seem to like him. But what about the *grandchildren*?"

The king laughed again, patting his wife's hand gently, "The boy's not fey, Miranda. Lord Flambére assures me he simply has an odd sense of humor. I thought he'd be a good match for our Jewel; she always did like a challenge."

Thessalyn led the prince out of the great hall and toward the gardens that filled nearly half the inner bailey. Once outside and away from the prying eyes of the court, Thessalyn stopped and turned to face the man who would be her husband.

Before she could speak, he reached out, lifted her off the ground by the waist and spun her in a full circle around him. "That was marvelous!" he exclaimed, "Just marvelous!"

Shocked and off balance, she grabbed his shoulders to steady herself and squeaked reflexively.

Noting her surprise, the prince's eyebrows raised, and he quickly set her back down, pulling his hands back to his chest, "Oh. Oh! I'm sorry. I should have asked. I forget that your people are less... physical than ours."

He tried to step back from her, but Thessalyn had kept her grip on his shoulders–and what firm shoulders they were. The rest of him seemed rather firm as well, the princess thought, dropping her gaze to the ground as she felt her cheeks heating.

"M-my lady?" Floriant asked frantically, trying to meet her eyes, but also unwilling to touch her again, "Are you well? Did I harm you?"

Thessalyn looked up, meeting his eyes and laughing, finally releasing his shoulders, albeit reluctantly, "Oh, you aren't going to be boring at all, are you?"

Floriant released a relieved sigh and sank to the ground, unconcerned by the dirt and grass that would surely stain his gown, "Thank the Stars. Mother would have killed me if I broke you. Seven Hells, *I'd* have killed me," he hit himself on the temple with the palm of his hand, and grumbled at himself, avoiding the princess' gaze, "That was stupid Flint. You must be more careful; your bride is *fragile*."

Thessalyn arranged her skirts and sat carefully before the large man, "I'm not that fragile," she said carefully, "and I'm quite well, you just... surprised me."

She reached out gingerly, lifting the prince's chin until he met her gaze. She gasped a little as his eyes met hers. Never had she seen eyes of such a rich brown, and she found herself captivated. For a moment, she felt like she was looking into the heart of a mountain, and, as she watched, his eyes seemed almost to glow and brighten with hues of gold. Just as quickly, the feeling was gone, and his eyes were that rich, earthy brown again.

Floriant relaxed a little as the woman before him smiled warmly. He tried to smile back at her but found that he was still shaking slightly from the fear that he had inadvertently damaged her.

He tipped his head slightly and reached out to push an escaped curl back from her face. She blushed, pinks and reds cascading across her delicate features, and he found himself released from his fear. "I am relieved that you are well. But you *are* quite fragile, I'm afraid, and I am much stronger than I look."

Thessalyn looked over the well-muscled man before her and raised an eyebrow, "My lord, I have eyes. I was not surprised that you *could* lift me, merely that you elected to do so."

Floriant smiled at the princess, laughing a little, "I, too, know how I look, but still you must understand that I am much stronger than I appear."

"So... West Rodanthian princes don't just live in the mountains, they lift mountains too?" Thessalyn giggled.

The prince stifled a laugh. "Indeed. But... there really *are* things you must know about me before we wed." Floriant's smile grew sad, and his tone turned serious. "I fear that I cannot explain everything today, but know that I shall not marry you while you are ignorant of my nature or the impact it may have on our union. I shall hold no secrets from you. I only hope that when the moon rises next month, you will still look so kindly upon me and our marriage."

Thessalyn nodded, confused but unsure what to ask for clarification.

Floriant shook his head and stood abruptly, reaching down to the princess. "Enough time for all that later," he said briskly as he pulled the girl easily to her feet, "Now, tell me about these plants! I was raised on the side of a mountain, you know, we don't get trees and shrubbery like this!"

'I—of course, my lord," Thessalyn replied, her mind still wondering what secrets he was keeping right now, but opting to follow his lead as he turned toward the gardens.

"Ooh!" The tall man exclaimed, "Are those *hedges*?! I've never seen one in person!"

"Yes. In fact, the gardeners have just finished trimming the maze for the spring festival. Would you like to see it?"

Floriant's face lit up like a midsummer bonfire, "A *HEDGE MAZE*?! This place is marvelous!"

And with that, the prince took Thessalyn's hand in his, grabbed his skirt with the other and flounced off toward the hedges, a surprised, but smiling, princess in tow.

"Father?" Thessalyn inquired as she slid into the king's office later that day.

"Yes, my Jewel?" her father smiled and set aside the stack of papers he'd been reviewing.

Her face took on a determined look as she strode in and sat in one of the heavily upholstered chairs across from the ancient wooden desk.

"Why didn't you tell me the treaty with West Rodanthia included a marriage clause?"

The king's smile wavered slightly, but then he shook his head and met his daughter's seeking eyes. He clasped his hands pensively before him and sighed lightly. "We were, honestly, a bit concerned that you wouldn't show up if you knew about the betrothal."

Thessalyn stared at her father, shocked. "Did you think I would not do my duty?"

Her father raised a wry eyebrow, "Jewel, you have turned down every suitor who has graced our door. Several before they even reached the door, if I recall. What would you have us think?"

Thessalyn opened her mouth to retort and then closed it, thinking over what her father had said. "I see. But Father, those were all met under the pretense of a potential love match. I've always understood that my position came with the possibility of a political marriage."

The king began to relax his grip cautiously.

"Besides," she continued, "Prince Floriant seems quite... *interesting*." Thessalyn turned away slightly, trying to hide her blush.

The older man laughed suddenly, "Ha! I knew he was the right one!"

Thessalyn cocked her head inquisitively toward her father.

"Oh, you should have seen his brothers," the king elaborated, relaxing into his chair and the comfortable rhythms their conversations typically followed, "I interviewed three of the sons, you know, the others were both ready to 'do their duty' and 'sacrifice their futures' for the good of the alliance."

Thessalyn rolled her eyes as her father mimicked the type of noble she'd turned down time and again.

"But Floriant," he smiled, recalling the conversation, "he asked about you. 'What is the princess like?' 'Does she enjoy reading, or riding?' 'Do you think I would suit her?'"

The princess found herself blushing harder as her father recounted the interaction. "He was not concerned about leaving his home to become the consort of a *foreign queen?*" her voice grew slightly sharp, recalling interactions she had had with past suitors.

Her father leaned forward, "Indeed not. What did he say? 'Are not the people more important than the place in a marriage?' Besides," he added, dropping his voice to a conspiratorial whisper, "Floriant is sixth in line for the crown in the west; he has never expected to rule. I rather think he was excited at the prospect of building a life somewhere new."

"Where shall you take the prince today, Your Highness?" Liana asked as she plaited Thessalyn's hair into an intricate, but modest braid.

"I thought we'd go down to the Merchant Quarter, perhaps visit the textile markets.

"Textiles, Your Highness?" Liana raised an eyebrow.

"Did you not hear, Liana? My betrothed is an award-winning *quilter.*"

"Surely not!" Liana exclaimed in disbelief, "I thought Edwin must be teasing me with such claims."

"Five-time champion, it seems," the princess' eyes danced with laughter as she explained, "Apparently, he donates the prize money to the local widows and orphans purse. I've been meaning to ask him more about it, and what better time than on a tour of our finest local textiles?"

"Indeed," the maid replied as she finished the current braid and moved to the next.

"I think we'll also stop by the Pear and let him meet some of the locals," Thessalyn continued, "I get the impression that his family is much more hands-off with their constituents than we are."

"Few rulers are quite so hands-on as your family, Highness," Liana mused, while layering the plaits together, "my cousins over in Balmeria have only ever seen their king once and have certainly never met the royal family."

They were interrupted by a firm knock, "Your Highness?" a masculine voice inquired.

"Enter," Liana replied brusquely, "we're nearly finished."

The door opened and Badgeford stepped inside, the glimmer of a smile making his eyes sparkle. "I've arranged your route, Highness: visiting three of the most popular and three of the most obscure textile and fabric merchants in the city."

"Excellent." Thessalyn smiled into the mirror and gathered her skirts to rise.

Floriant was polite, but clearly not impressed, with the most popular merchants. He chatted with them about the quality of their fabrics and the vibrancy of their patterns, but it was, overall, uneventful.

When they stepped into Holden's House of Hodden and Hosiery, however, the prince lit right up. Thessalyn smiled to herself as Floriant looked about and then headed straight for a collection of vividly colored bolts in the far corner of the shop. Bright and animated, Floriant was a stark difference from the types of nobles she had been raised with—all quiet, reserved, and all too often deceptive in their calmness. Floriant's face beamed with humor and personality, and this intrigued her.

Many men had paid her suit, from arrogant princes who felt she was beneath them, for all that she would be queen and none of them would ever rule in their own lands, to rich merchants' sons who sought to improve their station in her bed. But most of her suitors attempted to hide their ulterior motives. The few who hadn't, well, they'd been so dull, she may as well have courted the statues in the mausoleum. This prince was different: he had so much personality, he could barely contain it, even when prudence and propriety demanded a more reserved demeanor. That personality was not to be contained today, it seemed, as he called for the shopkeeper.

"Is this hand-dyed, Neithian silk?" he exclaimed, fingers sliding gently across the delicate fabric.

"You have a most discerning eye, my lord," Holden, the proprietor, agreed proudly, "I am the only licensed dealer of genuine Neithian silk in the east."

"Undyed, this is the brightest of whites, is it not?" Floriant asked.

"Indeed, it is, my lord."

"Have you any right now? It is so difficult to find true white in fine fabrics."

"Indeed, my lord, one of our specialties is custom dyes. How much do you need?"

Floriant waved for Thessalyn to come closer. "May I measure you, my lady? I should like to use this fabric for your bridal sash."

The princess stepped toward Floriant, nodding, "Bridal sash?"

"A tradition among my people," he smiled, reaching forward to lift her arms away from her waist. He pulled a compact measure from a pocket, and began draping the line quickly about her waist, hips, shoulders, and to the floor.

"Can I give you measurements in meters?" Floriant asked the proprietor.

"Of course, my lord."

"Then I should like..." he paused, calculating, "perhaps four meters? Is this standard meter-width? Twice that if it's half-meter width..."

The shopkeeper's eyes widened, "Yes, my lord. This cloth is half-meter width, so eight meters? It will be, ah, 48 gold crowns for eight meters, my lord."

Thessalyn's eyes also widened at the price, but Floriant simply nodded and reached for his purse, "Yes, of course."

"Have you need of a tailor, my lord?" Holden asked as he accepted the prince's payment.

"Certainly not!" Floriant exclaimed with mock horror, continuing with a broad grin, "I don't know how things are done here, but in the west, a groom takes pride in making the bridal gift by his own hand."

Arrangements were made for the prince's order to be delivered, and they continued to the remaining shops, where he procured a variety of exotic threads and chatted happily with the shopkeepers.

They finally arrived at the final stop of their tour: the Misty Pear.

The exterior of the Misty Pear was much like any other inn or tavern in town, a quaint building with an exterior falling into mild disrepair. A large, hand-painted sign hung above the entrance, displaying a tankard and a pear knocking together in celebration.

As they entered the tavern, Floriant took in the main room and its occupants quickly, noting the exits and checking the crowd for signs of weapons, while his own hand rested on the blade he carried. While West Rodanthia was on excellent terms with its closest neighbor, they had experienced more than a few unpleasant encounters with other nearby countries, leaving them with a long tradition of defense.

Thessalyn led them into the bustling crowd and caught the bartender's attention. He smiled broadly and pointed them to a large, empty table in the center of the room. She led the prince to the table and sat beside him, while Badgeford took a seat across from them.

"Should we have so large a table to ourselves?" the prince asked quietly, noticing the crowd of people standing about, while their table would easily seat eight or ten more. He expected the townspeople to give them space, but nothing about Thessalyn or her father had given him the impression that they would demand this level of accommodation.

"Oh no," Thessalyn said, with a twinkle in her eye, "They're just waiting for us to get settled."

Sure enough, not two breaths after the bartender had set down their drinks, the townsfolk began meandering closer, waiting for a nod from the herald, and then filling in the open seats on the benches, though they were careful to leave the space directly beside Thessalyn empty.

"I hear they finally found you a husband, Your Highness," a portly man teased the princess loudly from across the table, though his tone sounded friendly enough to Floriant.

"Heard His Grace had to sign a whole treaty to convince someone to wed her!" a female voice called in response from near the bar.

Floriant tensed beside the princess, feeling, again, confused by the culture and debating whether he should be leaping to her defense. In the west, one didn't speak out against those in power—at least not within earshot of them. His hand drifted toward the seemingly decorative knife on his belt, but before he'd decided whether to take action, the young woman next to him shot back.

"Four more weeks until the wedding, Jasper," Thessalyn's voice rang clearly above the crowd, "I still might scare him off!"

This was met by a chorus of cheerful laughter, and Jasper signaled his surrender with a raised tankard and a good-natured smile.

Floriant slowly relaxed into the casual atmosphere of the tavern, marveling at the easy chatter between the townspeople and the woman who would become their queen. He couldn't imagine such an interaction in the capital back home. The locals in the west found the royal family to be... intimidating. He answered questions from around the room about his people and West Rodanthia, while the princess chatted genially with folk about their families, crops, and everything else.

"That's right, we are known for our sheep in the west–our ranchers produce the finest mutton and wool on the continent," he told a young man who was, apparently, looking to improve his own flock's wool.

He found himself laughing at a barmaid's assertion that she's heard the western royals lived inside a live volcano, "No, not *inside* the volcano. Though one of my ancestors did build the keep off the side of it. Of course," he grinned, "they also say we're fireproof."

This brought a laugh from the crowd and caused Thessalyn to turn a beaming smile toward him. It struck him suddenly that he could very well see that smile every day soon, and he realized that his initial fondness for the princess could easily deepen into more. He was working through these thoughts, sipping on the last of his ale, when the woman in question mentioned asking the bartender for something, and, as if it were the most natural thing in the world, placed her hand on his thigh to brace herself as she stood.

Floriant froze, shocked both by the sudden, intimate contact and the way his heart had started racing when she touched him, and completely involuntarily clenched his hands into fists. When he heard Thessalyn's gasp, he remembered that he was holding a tankard, or at least he had been. Now, he found his right hand gripped around the crushed remains of the tankard.

Turning to face her, he saw the princess' eyes were wide with... surprise? Or was that fear?

"I—er..." Floriant fumbled for words, praying that look was just surprise. It had only been two weeks; when had he become so invested in how she perceived him?

It was Badgeford who broke the silence, making an almost comical show of inspecting his own cup, "I'd heard you West Rodanthians were strong, but, damn, are you sure you're a prince and not a blacksmith?!"

Floriant laughed nervously, finally releasing the crumpled cup into his lap, "Actually, my whole family are trained metalsmiths—I made the blade I'm wearing now." He shot the herald a grateful smile as he pulled the knife in question off his belt to show to the table. He relaxed further when Thessalyn gave his shoulder a comforting squeeze before continuing her quest to the bar.

The crowd was quickly distracted by the finely made blade the prince showed off, the conversation turning toward differences in tradecrafts between their countries.

Thessalyn made her way toward the bar, her heart still racing with surprise. Floriant had told her that he was stronger than he looked, but many men exaggerated their strength, so she'd thought nothing of it at the time. But he'd crushed that tankard with his bare hand. She'd once seen a man throw one of these cups full force against a stone wall and it had survived with hardly a dent.

She made a mental note to prioritize finding an opportunity to speak to her betrothed alone. He had clearly not been joking or embellishing when he'd said his family was different, and it was becoming clear that she really did need to understand what that meant before the wedding.

Her herald had diffused the situation smoothly—Badgeford was proving himself quite intuitive and effective in his role—but Thessalyn still took a few moments longer than necessary conversing with the bartender and composing herself before returning to the table. It was important that her people, and her betrothed, saw none of her doubts.

"I still don't see why the ceremony has to take place at *night*," Thessalyn's mother complained in a whining tone that implied strongly that she expected this to change.

"Two thousand years of tradition, Your Grace." Floriant grumbled as he grimaced through what he hoped was a polite smile, trying to explain to the queen *again* that this was very important, his willpower grating against his urge to loom over the queen in an intimidating fashion until she acquiesced.

"But—" the queen's face scrunched up as she prepared to push back.

"*Miranda*," the king sighed dramatically at his wife, "this isn't *your* wedding, why don't we ask what the *bride* thinks? Hm?"

Thessalyn watched as her mother turned toward her, an expectant look on her face. Swallowing a laugh, the princess smiled at her parents and said, "Well, as this is not merely a marriage between two people, but two kingdoms, two cultures even, I think we should include the most important aspects of *both* our wedding traditions."

Her mother's eyes took on a victorious glint, but Thessalyn continued quickly, before she could make another argument, "And, since none of *our* traditions speak to the time of day, I think it's perfectly reasonable to hold the ceremony at the time dictated by, what was it, *two-thousand years* of tradition? from my groom's culture."

Floriant sighed with relief and sat heavily beside Thessalyn, "Thank you. Yes. Correct timing is essential in all of our most important ceremonies and traditions."

"Now," Thessalyn turned her attention toward Floriant and continued, "what customs are important for West Rodanthian weddings?"

"Only three are required," Floriant began, "First and most important: the lighting and planting of the Ironwood. Don't fret," he assured them, "I prepared a tree before I left home. It shall arrive with my family's convoy."

Thessalyn tried to conceal her surprise as her betrothed mentioned the Ironwood, which, until this moment, she had believed to be myth or, at the very least, extinct.

"Ironwood blooms only beneath a full moon," Floriant explained apologetically, "This is why the ceremony can only be held beneath a full moon in ascendance.

"Ah," Thessalyn replied, an idea forming, "It is this lighting of the tree that must happen beneath the full moon, then?" and was rewarded with an affirmative nod from the prince.

"Then there we have it," Thessalyn smiled happily as if her mother's ears had not begun to emanate smoke, "we'll hold the ceremony, oh, our traditions include a handfasting as part of the ceremony, will that conflict...?" she paused to receive a confirming shake of the head from her betrothed, "excellent. We'll hold the handfasting, per our traditions, late in the evening and then perform the Ironwood ceremony beneath the full moon, per my groom's traditions, and won't it just be lovely?"

Thessalyn's mother, accepting her daughter's compromise on the matter, finally sat beside her husband and resisted the urge to voice further opinions, though she didn't look happy about it.

"You mentioned three customs?" the princess asked.

"Yes," Floriant continued, "second, the bride and groom are to exchange tokens, like the sash I am making for Her Highness."

The queen leaned forward urgently, her eyes widening with concern, "It-it doesn't have to be *stitched*, does it? Our daughter has many fine skills, but I fear the needle arts are not among them."

"Mother!" Thessalyn exclaimed, blushing with embarrassment as her father chortled.

"Oh, hush, dear," her mother waved dismissively, "He was going to find out sooner or later."

Floriant joined the king's laughter and reassured them, "No, no, the token can be anything, it simply must be made by her own hand and represent her positive intentions toward this union. *My* skills lend themselves to the sash, but my parents forged rings for each other, and I do believe one of my aunts painted a portrait of her betrothed's prized hunting hound. A few of us were concerned that he loved that dog more than her, but it all worked out in the end."

"So, I need to *make* a token for you?" Thessalyn confirmed, "to be presented to you during the ceremony?"

"Indeed," Floriant smiled at his bride, appreciating his luck that she was so amenable to his people's customs, "And the third we've already discussed: the timing of the Ironwood ritual."

Thessalyn nodded, her mind beginning to turn on what type of token she could make for the prince, particularly when she had never been particularly skilled at the making of, well, anything. But this was important, both to her future husband's culture, and, she was realizing, to her as well. She wanted to give Floriant something that showed him how she felt. She had realized that, for her at least, this wasn't just a political marriage anymore. Floriant had found a home in her heart with his easy smile and his kind demeanor. Her token would be something that showed him that he had won her heart.

Deciding that she needn't choose this instant, she turned her focus back to the issue at hand and asked, "Are there any timing restrictions for other aspects of the celebration? The banquet, the tour, and such?"

"Tour?" Floriant asked.

"Ah, you don't do a wedding tour?" she laughed lightly at the prince's confused expression, "One of our traditions, specifically for royal weddings, is for the new couple to tour the city after the wedding, meeting with the people and giving small gifts to the local children. Events on this scale tend to disrupt the whole city and we like to make sure the people know that we notice. This is typically followed by a longer tour of the kingdom, where we'll visit all cities and most towns to meet with the people across East Rodanthia. The whole endeavor tends to take about six months or so."

The prince's confusion melted into a small smile, "You engage with your people much more directly than we do in the west; it is... refreshing. The tour, the banquet, schedule those as you like, so long as they do not interfere with the ceremony." His smile widened into a grin, "I'm rather looking forward to the banquet, actually; I hear your mother's banquets are quite spectacular."

Miranda blushed at the sudden compliment, "Oh, hardly," she waved her hand dismissively at Floriant, but anyone could tell she was pleased, "Just a little food, a little music, nothing to get so excited about. But we should discuss the menu, shouldn't we?"

The queen, appeased and ready to plan the banquet of the century, began naming off popular and exotic dishes featuring beef, pork, and various fish. She stopped suddenly and turned to Floriant, "Oh! Goodness. I don't know much about foods from the west, your family aren't... *vegetarians*, are they?"

Floriant stared incredulously at the queen, "Ve-vegetarian?" He laughed deeply and shook his head, "No, Your Grace, we are not vegetarians. Rather partial to mutton, actually."

"Oh, thank the stars." the queen exhaled in relief and continued, "Mutton? Oh, I-I'm sure our chef can come up with something..."

The king smiled and added, "I believe Lord Flambére mentioned that they would be bringing a flock and one of their cooks to assist with the banquet, isn't that right?"

"Indeed, Your Grace," Floriant agreed with a twinkle in his eye, "West Rodanthia boasts the finest sheep farmers on the continent, and we thought this an appropriate *bride price* for me." He laughed and turned his attention to the queen, "Our cook will, of course, defer to your chef in regard to the banquet, but we thought it would be easier to bring someone who can prepare a few of our favorite dishes, rather than simply sending recipes."

"Yes, of course," Miranda agreed.

Everyone settled in comfortably as the queen began planning the wedding banquet with gusto.

Floriant paced nervously in the trees. It had been, unsurprisingly, difficult to get the princess alone, but they'd finally found a time when she could step away unescorted. With the wedding only two weeks away, and his family already en route, he knew this would be his only chance to ensure that Thessalyn knew who, and what, he really was.

He knew what he had to do, had to say, but now that the time had come, he was worried about how she might respond, though all their interactions thus far had led him to believe that she was of strong enough spirit not to let such a matter as this interfere with the wedding plans.

But that was the problem, wasn't it? He'd gotten to know the princess and had found himself liking her so much more than he had expected.

He had prepared himself for a political marriage: amenable to begin, companionable with time, and had hoped that the princess and he would suit well enough that the union wasn't a chore.

He had been wholly unprepared for the spark she lit in his heart, the way her smiles released butterflies in his stomach, the way he longed to touch her.

If she rejected him now... no, he couldn't think about that. All he could do was be honest with her and let the cards fall where they may.

Thessalyn slowed her steed as she approached the clearing atop the nearest of the western foothills. She noticed, not for the first time, how the landscape grew taller and taller as it approached the border, where the mountains of the west began. She dismounted and tethered the grey horse where it could graze.

She walked around the clearing, taking in the sight of the valley that lay back the way she'd come. Her home was beautiful, and this was the best spot in all of East Rodanthia to view the whole capital city with its sprawling buildings and gardens.

Looking back around the empty clearing, she wondered if she was in the right place. There was no sign that another rider had been through this way recently, but hadn't Floriant told her that he'd come here often since his arrival?

The princess needn't have worried, because the man in question came striding out of the woods a few minutes later. His face lit up when he saw her, and she couldn't help smiling herself. She'd found herself smiling quite often since the prince's arrival.

"My lady!" he exclaimed happily, "I hope I haven't kept you waiting?" He jogged easily across the clearing to meet her.

"Mere moments, my lord." She took his offered hands, "you-you wished to speak with me?"

Floriant nodded and squeezed her hands gently, "Yes. I told you when first we met, that there were things you needed to know about me, you recall?"

She nodded, wondering about the man's nervousness. Floriant had shown little but confidence, charm, and a striking sense of humor in their time together. There had been a few odd moments, sure, but she'd never seen him off kilter like this. She realized that another woman might have felt concerned in this situation, being asked to meet with a man in secret and then finding him acting strangely when there were no others nearby to witness. But her instincts told her that she was safe, and her experience, short though it may be, with the man before her told her that he harbored no ill intentions toward her.

"Good. Good. I, well, you see, we—" he released her hands and took a step back.

Thessalyn waited, hoping her smile was an encouraging one. This was clearly very important to him, and she didn't want to make him more nervous than he already was.

He ran a hand awkwardly through his thick hair and smiled bashfully at her, "I didn't think this would be so difficult. Perhaps I should have insisted on this conversation earlier, before I was so invested, but," the smile faded, "I was afraid..."

"Afraid of what?" Thessalyn asked gently, though she couldn't imagine the man before her being afraid of anything.

Floriant smiled again, but sharply, "That you wouldn't want me," he sighed again, dropping his gaze to the ground, "after I told you the truth; that you'd fear me."

Thessalyn stepped forward and, impulsively, lifted his chin until he met her eyes, "How could I fear such a kind man?"

Gold flecks blossomed across his irises until the eyes that looked back at Thessalyn were no longer the rich brown to which she'd grown accustomed. She'd seen the gold peek out before but had always thought it to be her imagination or a trick of the light. This time, however, there was no denying the change she beheld. Her own eyes widened as he tore himself away from her grip and growled, "And what if I weren't a *man* at all?"

Thessalyn stood frozen, her arm still raised, as she watched her betrothed battle his emotions. She would never admit it to him, but in this moment, she was feeling the beginnings of fear. "My lord?" she asked softly, "I don't understand..."

Floriant turned away from her and took a deep, shaking breath. "I'm sorry. I'm doing this all wrong."

He turned back to her and smiled sadly, but his eyes, brown again, looked resolved as he spoke, "My people, my family, are different. I've told you some, and you've witnessed my strength, but it's not just that we are stronger than you," he wrung his hands together nervously, which only further emphasized the strength in his arms, and continued, "there is magic in our blood, ancient earth magic that makes us what we are. I—" he paused thoughtfully, and his face fell, "I don't know that you'll believe me if I don't show you."

"Then show me," Thessalyn said, feeling her temper beginning to rise in response to Floriant's erratic behavior and wandering speech.

"What?!"

"If it must be seen to be believed, then show me."

Floriant's eyes widened, but he nodded. "Stay there, this—I need more space."

He stepped backward until he was roughly centered in the clearing, clenching and releasing fists with both hands as he went. He looked around to confirm the space, then met the princess' eyes, gave her a sad but hopeful smile, and *changed*.

The air around Floriant began to shift and shimmer as if an

excess of heat was emanating from him. After a moment, Thessalyn could no longer see the man clearly, his visage had blurred into the shimmering air. The sight made her slightly dizzy, so she found herself averting her gaze.

When she looked back, bright gold eyes caught hers. Floriant's gold eyes, she knew, but her waking mind wasn't yet ready to make that connection.

Surrounding those eyes were hundreds of tiny bronze and copper scales.

She gasped in surprise and took an involuntary step back as her brain struggled to catch up with her eyes. Small comments and odd moments from their courtship began to fall into place as she tried to reconcile what she was seeing against her knowledge of the world.

The creature before her was massive, filling half the clearing with scales and claws, limbs as thick as tree trunks, and wings. The wings were captivating: iridescent membranes stretched between copper spines; she watched them flex and stretch before settling in against his back.

The creature before her, the *dragon* her mind insisted, saw her hesitation and shrank back from her in response, seemingly trying to make himself smaller.

They stood there unmoving for a moment, or several hours, surely, if one were to ask Floriant, until Thessalyn broke the silence.

"Oh, Flint," she whispered, forgetting formalities as she took in the wonder before her, "You're beautiful."

She stepped forward slowly until she was mere inches away from him. At her wave, he lowered his head slowly toward the ground, watching her cautiously with those great gold eyes. Thessalyn placed her hands gently on his nose, finding to her surprise that the scales were quite soft as she ran fingers calmly up his snout. She leaned forward and kissed his nose lightly, then whispered with a small smile as she stepped back, "I just *knew* you wouldn't be boring."

The air shimmered around them again, and this close she could feel the heat in the magic. A moment later, her betrothed, looking surprised and flustered, but otherwise just like himself, stood before her. He reached out, brushing a stray curl away from her face and then touching her cheek tentatively, as if he feared she would disappear, his eyes searching her face. "You didn't run," he whispered, hope in his voice.

Thessalyn smiled and saw relief flood across the prince's features. She caught his gaze, marveling as his eyes wavered between brown and gold. She was beginning to wonder if the gold came out whenever his emotions ran high. She reached up and pressed his warm hand against her cheek and whispered back, "Why should I run from you?"

Floriant had closed the distance between them and leaned down to kiss her before he realized what he'd done. Thessalyn froze with surprise when his lips met hers, but when his brain caught up with him and he tried to pull away, he found her arms wrapping around his neck and her slim form pressing against him. Pushing down the panic and his mother's stern voice reminding him that physical intimacies were for *after* the wedding in the east, Floriant lost himself in the kiss, in Thessalyn's soft lips, her possessive embrace, the vibration of her racing heartbeat, if only for a moment.

Finally, and much too soon, if one were to ask Thessalyn, Floriant pulled back, breaking the connection. His bride stood before him with heat in her eyes, her skin flushed, and the beginnings of a wicked smile curling the corner of her lips. It took more willpower than he'd expected to not immediately take her back into his arms, to not taste those lips again.

"It seems that you are full of surprises today, my lord," her voice trembled slightly, and, having rediscovered the proprieties of her station, she blushed somehow more and dropped her gaze from him.

"Surprises all around, it seems," Floriant rumbled gently, his heart finally easing from anxiety toward joy.

The handfasting was held just before sunset.

Unlike the bridal gown Prince Floriant had worn at their first meeting, Thessalyn's gown was a complicated affair of fabrics and supportive boning. White and silver layers danced around each other, while green accents wove their way throughout. Much to the queen's relief, the groom had opted for a more traditional look, with a shimmering copper doublet layered over a fine white shirt and matching copper trousers tucked tidily into tall black boots.

They stood facing each other, framed dramatically by an extravagant floral arch, angled so the setting sun would sink through the center of the arch between them. White star jasmine blossomed off the vines that created the frame of the arch, with copper irises and orange butterfly ranunculus scattered throughout to create a palette that complimented the couple's attire.

They recited the traditional vows, speaking of loyalty to each other and duty to the kingdom, much as one would hear at any other royal wedding. As they finished, Thessalyn's father and Floriant's mother approached from their respective sides to deliver the ceremonial gifts.

Floriant's mother handed him a carefully folded bundle. He loosed the parcel to reveal the lengthy sash he had fashioned over the past month. He smiled bashfully at his bride as he draped the bright white fabric from her right shoulder to her left hip. He knelt before her and fastened the sash to her gown with an ornate silver clip where the delicate fabric overlapped at her hip then brought the fabric around to her other hip where he fastened it again with a matching clip. He released the tails of the sash, and they flowed gently toward the ground, ending near the princess' ankles.

As her groom wrapped her in his gift, Thessalyn marveled at the elegant embroidery that traveled the length of the garment. Hand-stitched vines wandered from one end to the other in a pale, shimmering green, while dozens of tiny copper dragons danced around the vines. Subtle iridescent flowers and curls accented the remaining space, creating a sense of whimsy across the piece.

Floriant rose and reached for Thessalyn's hands. He brought her hands to his lips and kissed them gently. He was rewarded with a radiant smile when she met his eyes as he released her hands.

Thessalyn accepted her own small bundle from her father and turned her attention back to her groom and whispered. "I fear that my gift is not nearly so fine as yours, but I did plait it with my own hands."

Her cheeks flushed with embarrassment as she opened the cloth to show Floriant a long, braided cord. "The green threads are linen made from the finest local flax," she explained, "to tie you to our land. The white yarns are spun from the wool of the sheep your family brought, to tie you to your home.

"The brown—" she swallowed nervously before continuing, "the brown is my own hair, spun in with the wool, to tie you to me. And I stitched a copper thread throughout, to reinforce the plait, and to tie us to each other."

Floriant ran his fingers along the cord, feeling the twists and layers of the braid. He smiled as he found the bumps and imperfections that were causing his bride to blush. "It's perfect," he reassured her, "Thank you."

Thessalyn sighed with relief and relaxed visibly. When she nodded, her father stepped forward and completed the handfasting ceremony, binding the bride's right hand to the groom's left with the cord that Thessalyn had so carefully crafted.

As the first full moon of spring neared its zenith above them, the couple stood before the Ironwood sapling that Floriant had prepared. Floriant's family stood to one side of the ornate pot, while Thessalyn's stood to the other.

The tree was small, shorter than Floriant but slightly taller than Thessalyn. It resembled an oak or maple sapling with its thick truck and spindly, reaching branches. It was beautiful, though it bore no leaves or fruit, its dark, metallic bark glistening gently in the moonlight.

Floriant stood behind her, wrapping his arms around her smaller frame and catching her hands in his. He wore their handfasting cord wrapped down his left forearm like a bracer. Thessalyn felt her heart beat faster at his closeness and she resisted the urge to lean back against him.

"We must summon the Sacred Flame—the power of my people, passed down from our Father, the great Fire, and our Grandmother, the Sun." Floriant's deep voice rumbled gently against her neck.

"I can't summon fire—" she whispered, hoping silently that he didn't believe she could.

Floriant stifled a small laugh, "Tonight, with my help, and the blessings of our ancestors, you can." His reassuring words carried his smile, "we'll summon the Flame and give it to our tree. If our union is accepted, we will be blessed with the fruit of the Ironwood."

He formed a bowl with their layered hands, curved and open to the sky, and spoke, "Grandmother," his clear voice projected to all in attendance, "I bring to you my bride, my love, she who holds the flame of my heart. Grant me the Fire that our love may burn for a lifetime."

Thessalyn felt the power in his words as they echoed around her. In the air above her open palms, a spark burst into being. She twitched in surprise, but Floriant's strong hands held hers steady.

"Grandmother," she began and felt the strange power ripple through her as she spoke the words she'd memorized, "I bring to you my groom, my love, he who holds the flame of my heart. Grant me the Fire that our love may burn for a lifetime."

The spark began to spin lazily, but no flames appeared. Worried, she began to turn, to ask what was wrong, but Floriant squeezed her hands gently.

"Shh. Be patient. It will come in its own time."

Thessalyn froze, holding her hands steady and watching the gently turning spark in wonder.

After what felt like a lifetime, but her father assured her later had been mere moments, the spark blossomed into flame. Tiny blue fronds rippled from the glowing ball.

"Oh," she couldn't contain her wonder, "it's beautiful." She whispered.

Quiet murmurs from Floriant's family caught her attention, and her worry returned.

"Don't mind them," he whispered, "they're just surprised we got blue," Thessalyn heard laughter and was that pride? in his voice.

"Is blue unusual?" she whispered, still concerned that she had somehow done something wrong.

"Hardly. Though most arranged unions do see red," he whispered back.

"Then why—"

"Later." He cut her off gently, "We must release the Flame."

Thessalyn closed her mouth and nodded, ready to follow his lead through the remainder of the ritual.

He lifted their hands slowly toward the Ironwood sapling that stood, small and proud, before them. The ball of writhing flames moved with them, always remaining suspended in the space above their cupped hands.

"Give to the Flame your hopes and dreams for our future together," he whispered as he held their hands and the flames aloft for a moment, "and then..."

He pulled her hands apart and away from the Flame and then pushed gently. The Flame shivered and then floated lazily toward the tree. Never releasing her hands, Floriant wrapped his arms loosely around her waist and leaned his head over her shoulder so they could watch the flame's progress together.

Thessalyn found herself holding her breath as the fire approached the Ironwood. The tiny ball stopped as it touched the trunk of the sapling and then sunk slowly into the heart of the tree. Soon it was gone, and the tree looked, well, exactly as it had before.

She continued to hold her breath, unsure whether everything was working as it should, but unwilling to ask again about the ceremony. Floriant continued to watch the tree intently from over her shoulder—was he also holding his breath?

A full eternity later, if one were to ask any of those in attendance, the Ironwood tree bloomed spectacularly.

The tip of each branch began to glow a pale, shimmery white, then bright blue leaves sprung to life from every branch, sprouting and unfurling as if spring had come suddenly to this tree in particular. As Thessalyn looked closer, she saw the leaves were made of the same flame they had held moments ago.

Floriant's family began to clap and cheer, with Thessalyn's joining the celebration a moment or two later. Floriant exhaled and finally withdrew his arms from around her. He caught her hand and squeezed it gently as their families came toward them.

One of Floriant's brothers rushed forward and caught him in an aggressive hug, "Never thought I'd see a blue Flame for this one," he teased, sending a wink toward Thessalyn, "Did he win you over with his needlepoint?"

Thessalyn giggled at Floriant's suddenly embarrassed expression but replied seriously, "Oh, yes, you can't imagine the years I've spent longing for a man with stitchery skills."

The teasing man's eyebrows shot up in surprise then dropped as he laughed, releasing Floriant, "Oh, I like her, brother. She'll keep you on your toes."

"A love match!" Lady Ember exclaimed before Floriant could reply, "We're so happy for you!" She gathered Thessalyn into a gentle hug. "My lovely new daughter," she whispered, "Flint has assured me that you are aware of our family's... nature, but you may find you have questions better answered by a woman. Please know that I am at your disposal."

Thessalyn hugged her mother-in-law gratefully and replied, "Thank you. I expect I shall have many questions."

Thessalyn pried herself gently away from the hug and caught her husband's hand in hers. She looked up at Floriant and reveled for a moment in this bright spark of a man who had become hers, then she squeezed his hand and led him toward her parents and the toasts that both their fathers had prepared.

A KIND OF MAGIC

Johnny Roach

So we ran, Amber picking a direction at each junction, apparently at random to throw off the guards looking for us. We made enough ground to lose them in the mansion's hallways, and she picked one last door.

I pulled it open, grunting to get her attention. She came back from the corner she was peering around and looked in. It was a study, lined with bookshelves and filled with overstuffed chairs and, most importantly, a window that opened onto the alley below.

She slid in, and I followed. I found a heavy cabinet filled with bottles of wine and slid it in front of the door. "That should buy us a minute—"

That's when her heel shattered the little square plate set in the middle of the room.

Sometimes, when I'm lying down at night and my eyes drift off, my whole body jolts like I've slipped off a three-story building and slammed onto the street below. Maybe that's why they call it falling asleep.

But when the trap went off—some sort of gravity spell—I did fall. Flat on my back. The impact knocked the wind out of me, and

I gasped until my lungs were full again.

"It worked, you know."

My head throbbed where it had smashed into the floor. "Yeah, we're pinned down real good, Amber. Rather wish it hadn't, to be honest."

I don't know how magical runes work. "The art either reveals itself to you or it doesn't," an Artificer I worked with told me once. But I do know you can either shape the magic by some sort of recitation or let it erupt by setting it free. Usually, this is done by containing the spell in thin wafers and cracking them like overcooked bacon. It was crude, and they cost a small fortune, but it made for a fun party trick. In this case, it made me feel like an entire warehouse of rugs had been dropped on me.

"Not that, Frank," she said. She was in front of me and like me was being pinned to the floor by the spell. I was on my back, her on her stomach. The trap held my head against the floor, but I could move my eyes. The door was behind me though, but I couldn't roll my eyes far enough to see it. "The love spell you put on me," she said. "I have to admit it worked."

Behind me, I heard muffled cries of "Over here!" The mansion was large enough that they would have to search room by room for us, and we were several stories up from the ballroom.

"When do you think I had time to put a love spell on you?" I strained my eyes downward to see her. Her brunette hair, braided up as part of her disguise, was still immaculate. I could see her face and shoulders—bare because of the dress—but nothing further. I had to force my eyes downward until I saw black spots to see her necklace, which thankfully wasn't choking her. She looked every part the lovely lady she was pretending to be for the spring ball. Her dress—red, flowing, and clingy—had taken my breath away when I'd first seen her in it, but I'd said only "That should work." In actuality, because the ball originated with some long-forgotten ritual pleading with dead gods for good crops and hearty children, it tended to devolve into an orgy, during which the dress would have made Amber very popular. But we'd tried to slink off during the ritualistic dance when we noticed hands slip down from the small of ladies' backs to their bottoms. Amber figured we'd have a few extra seconds of scouting around if everyone had to pull their unmentionables up before they realized we were gone. Of course, it would have worked better if she hadn't stepped on my toes hard enough for me to yelp.

"Maybe when we first met," she said. I heard her hands scratching but couldn't see what she was up to. I was also straining; I'd stashed a knife in a secret pouch in my sleeve. The trap only worked on larger muscles. Smaller ones, like the ones in fingers, were too fine for the trap to control without someone shaping the Essence into wispy tendrils to weave their way through them. Maybe I could curl my fingers up far enough to tug my knife out.

"First met? I was covered in soot and shit." I'd just infiltrated a guild storehouse through a chimney and exfiltrated through the sewer. She was panicking, but she didn't know about my secret sleeve knife.

"You're right. And a bit of a buffoon, now that I think about it. So the second time we met, later that night, after you'd bathed."

Kalkagos, my muscle, had brought her around about a year ago, saying she was a smooth talker and a hell of a lockpick. I gave her a shot.

"I needed you to open a safe, not swoon over me." The safe had come with me out of the storehouse and was almost as ripe as I was. I hadn't dared wash it in case that activated some tracking spell, so she had to work dirty.

"What makes you think I cast a spell on you?"

"Because I've opened that kind of safe a thousand times, and every time the crew leader would spend the entire time staring at either my front or my back. You handed me a rag soaked with perfume and told me to shove it up my nose and let me know when I was done. And you didn't call me 'Doll' even once."

"So?"

"So you were confident you'd have me sooner or later and didn't have to waste time leering at me while I worked."

She'd brought me the deeds from the safe five minutes later. She said it took her thirty seconds to get them and another four and a half minutes to finish dry-heaving. The next job, she went with us. She'd been with us ever since.

Footsteps echoed through the halls, but they could have been from either three stories or three feet away. My ear was pressed against the floor, so everything was amplified. I'd thought a guard was banging on the door, but that was just my heartbeat.

I couldn't turn my head to look for shadows passing by, but in my mind everyone in the mansion had their ear pressed against the door, listening for sounds of breathing. I hadn't been able to pull the dagger from my sleeve yet, but I kept working.

"Sorry to disappoint," I whispered, my eyes aching from trying to see behind me. "But I didn't cast any spells on you. If I'd had any skill with spell crafting that night, I would have used it to clean myself. That stuff was... everywhere."

I could hear her fingers still scrabbling at something. "If you get your hands free, slide the dagger out of my sleeve. I'll take out as many of them as I can to buy you time."

"What, and give up on getting this magical rune I've got stuffed up my bangle that is exactly what we need to get out of here?"

"What do you have stuffed up your bangle?" If she had ever displayed any competency in magic, I might have let myself hope. But her sense of humor far outstripped her skill in the art.

"This. Can you see it?" Even straining, I could only see down to her shoulder, and even that made me feel like my eyeballs were being wrenched from their sockets.

"You're giving me the finger, aren't you?" I said.

"Maybe."

"Well, use that one and the other four to get my blade, will you? It's our only chance." Getting the dagger was only the first step. I still had to get my hand free, then my arm, get her up and through the window, and fend everyone off so she could get away. She knew all this. I just wanted to give her some hope.

"To tell you the truth, it could have also been while we were dancing."

"Ah, the dancing. Let me think." My fingers were screaming in pain. "Couldn't have been then. I was too busy getting lost in the music. My hips are still swaying, see?" I nearly threw my back out trying to make my butt wiggle.

"Oh, is that what that was? I thought you were having a seizure. I had to clamp onto your hips to force you into something resembling a dance step."

"You were just trying to feel me up." I had vastly overestimated my readiness to pass as a court-trained dancer, while somehow Amber knew all of the steps. Well, almost all of them. That must be the sort of thing they discuss at parties while the rest of us are trying to drown ourselves at the bar.

"I won't deny you cut quite the figure in your little gentleman costume. But you apparently didn't look quite good enough to charm the guards." Her fingers stopped making noise. She wasn't wrong to give up. There was nothing we could do except hope they killed us here. The Baron had a nasty reputation for how he handled thieves, and I'd stolen from him twice already.

I laughed. "I haven't seen a room turn against a couple like that since that wedding you took Kalkagos to."

"At least at that one he'd pulled out a hammer and demanded all their jewelry, not just missed a couple of dance steps. Must be their national pastime." I heard frustration in her voice and maybe a touch of ... fear? I managed a glance at her face and saw that she was looking down at our hands.

"I'll get it," I said. "I'll save myself, and if you ask nicely, I'll think about saving you too." I smiled as I grunted, the sweat making my hands slick. My fingertips weren't even near the pocket. Eventually, the magic would wear off enough for me to reach the knife, but by then we'd be covered in pitch and hanging from the Baron's balcony. With luck, he wouldn't have skinned us first.

"By the time you stop screaming from my daring escape," she said, "Kalkagos and I will be halfway to the loot." Our eyes met and held for a beat, and she smiled. "Do try to keep up."

My hand started to ache, that strange, dull ache I get when I fold my thumb too far toward my elbow. I cried out a little bit, more in frustration than pain.

"I've narrowed it down then," she said.

"I prefer a simple 'Thank you, sir.'" I said, hissing through my teeth.

She snorted, almost silently. I'd heard her do that on enough jobs to know that if it had been anyone else, they would have been laughing so hard a cleric would have given them a touch of artisanal healing. "I'm sorry," she said after she caught her breath. "You prefer... what?"

"I assumed you were narrowing down how you would express your gratitude after my quick thinking rescued us at the last minute."

I'd made no progress on getting the sleeve knife, but at least I was now both trapped and aching from the effort.

"Right, right. Actually, I had narrowed down when you cast your love spell. But funny, it just wore off. Seems like there's not enough room in here for it and your ego." She gave me a hard look that lasted almost a full second before the glint returned to her eye.

"I'll bite," I said. "My rescue will be even more last-minute if I take a break to listen to your little story."

She cast her eyes down to our hands again, probably to ensure I was true to my word. "It was earlier today. When Kalkagos told you he was too sick to run the smash-and-grab plan."

"He's never been sick before. I didn't even know dwarves could get sick." They can't. He isn't. But there's some reason he couldn't do the job, some reason he can't tell me. But he's stuck with me all these years, so I stuck with him today.

"Oh, he's just debilitatingly drunk and too embarrassed to admit it. Imagine you'd drank too much to run a job. Now imagine you've got that legendary dwarven tolerance."

"Shame."

"The shame must have been the reagent. You saw his shame, held it in your hand, but instead of pressing him, of making it clear that you knew he just couldn't hold his liquor, you pretended to believe he was sick."

"He's a pro. If he says he's too sick to work, he's too sick to work. I've seen him take on an entire outpost with enough arrow wounds and booze in him to stop most armies."

"And you didn't yell, and you didn't call off the job. Instead, you asked me what I thought we should do. And when I told you I had a plan, you trusted me."

"I wanted to see if you could put together an operation, so I gave you a shot." I laughed. "But look around. Maybe I shouldn't have."

"Maybe," she said. I could see the shrug in her eyes. "Or maybe that was the absolute best choice you could have made." I giggled, and she laughed, but only after a beat. "But you trusted in your people, and there's a kind of magic to that."

I liked it when she laughed. Many nights at camp it was the only thing that kept me warm. I heard the guards storm into the room, then realized it was just my heart pounding again.

"I'm sorry," I said. "That I couldn't save us, I mean."

"You managed to barricade the door."

I tried to look behind me, but my neck still wouldn't budge. My eyes tilted in the right direction though, leaving me staring at the ceiling. "That only bought us a few minutes, Amber. You know that."

"I only need a few minutes. To tell you that I'm the one who's sorry." The poor woman had no fear in her voice. She must have already resigned herself.

"For what? It wasn't a bad plan, it just didn't play out the way you wanted."

"Not for the plan, you dolt. It was a great plan, and I've got them exactly where I want them. 'Surrounded from the inside,' I think it's called." I heard her fingers slide across something again.

"Then what are you sorry about?"

Behind me, I heard a crash that could only have been the wine cabinet being knocked over. The door burst open, and boots piled in, careful to stay far enough from the center of the room to avoid being trapped with us. I heard a curse uttered and a blade dropped behind me. Probably one of the guards drew his sword and discovered exactly how far the spell extended.

They called for an artificer, and I knew our time was up. "Amber," I said. "I didn't cast a love spell on you, but I do love you."

She looked me in the eyes and laughed. "I know you do, doofus."

Behind me, I heard the black cant of an artificer unwinding the trap's spell. Seconds now.

"Amber, if this is it, I think—"

She shushed me. "Don't think about them. They don't matter. It's just you and me, my love."

"But when they—" Suddenly I felt lighter. I took a deep breath, my chest freer than I could ever remember. Then I heard a tentative step, and I knew a confident one would be soon after. The foot had probably already been lifted.

"I said they don't matter, dummy. But I wanted to say I'm sorry I never figured out how to pronounce this incantation. So this is going to hurt."

I heard a snap, and everything went white. My mind exploded, shrieking in anger at... everything. The whole room turned itself inside out and shoved itself up my nose. I clenched my eyes tight to shut out the light, but the sound battered my brain like a piano falling down a flight of stairs. The cacophony got louder until even keeping my eyes closed was too much. I gave up and let them fall open.

By the time I realized we were back at the camp in the warehouse a few alleys over, Amber was already standing next to Kalkagos. I sat up, then lay back down just so I could sit up again. I never thought moving felt so good until I couldn't. "What happened?"

Amber barely turned her head over her shoulder to look at me. "What do you mean? I spent the entire time we were in there telling you I had a teleportation rune stuffed in my bangle. I couldn't get the incantation right, so I broke it."

Kalkagos nodded at me. "Sorry for deceiving you, my boy. She said she wanted to talk to you and so I should sit this one out." He chuckled. "I spent the entire time polishing off her bottle. Good stuff, A."

She clapped him on the back. "Lots more of that in the vault."

"But where did you get the rune? You can't afford that kind of kit!"

She scoffed. "I'm a thief. I stole it."

Kalkagos hefted his warhammer onto his shoulder. "So I take it the ballroom plan worked?" He asked, then tucked his smaller hammer—which he dubbed his "peacehammer" after a bottle or two—into his belt.

"Like a charm. Right about now, all of the guards are piling into an empty room in the west wing, and the militia they called for support are coming through the north gate."

Kalkagos whistled appreciatively. "Alas, here we are, southeast of the whole mansion, with no one between us and the loot."

"Alas." Amber walked over and pulled me to standing. I stared into her eyes, then to her lips, trying to figure out how much of this had been a prank. She must have caught me.

"After, lover." She passed me a sword from Kalkagos. "First, he smashes and we grab."

So we did. And then we did.

PLIGHT OF THE BIMBLPEAS

Jessica Brawner

Winter lingered longer than any of us wanted. The heavy snows pinned us in, blanketing the landscape in white and deadening sound, until it felt like we were the only ones left alive. In late March the first fuzzy Pasque flowers should have been visible on the mountain slopes, and the early crocuses should be poking their purple heads above the cold white blanket of snow. There was no sign of either.

It was only two weeks past her usual arrival date, but the severity of the winter made us anxious. Titania, Queen of Spring and Summer, in her cloak of flowers, hadn't arrived. Everyone was on edge; many were still asleep with the relentless cold. Wingtips were fragile, and the sap hadn't started flowing through our veins yet.

I limped down the inside of the hollow branch until I arrived at the meeting hall, my wingtips nearly frozen—the entire center of this enormous tree was hollowed out in such a way that it was big enough for the entire community to gather for meetings. Usually in the spring this was to dance and celebrate. No-one felt like celebrating now though. The forest elders had been clear. Everyone who wasn't ill, injured, or still hibernating must be at the meeting.

I settled down on one of the smaller branches, watching my fellow Fae arrive—there were fewer than I expected perhaps two dozen in total, when the hall normally held at least a hundred. The small grouping looked lost in the cavernous space, and with everyone's glimmer muted due to the cold, it was a cheerless gathering. Two close friends arrived, Hollybell and Lillipuff, both shivering in the cold. I flitted down to the center of the hall to meet them. As Titanias ladies in waiting, we were always amongst the first to awaken in spring.

Elder Makin had been the leader of the elders for as long as I remembered. He was a gruff, and gnarled with age, and looked like an old twisted bit of knotty pine as he stood in center stage.

"Fairies of Bimblpea—quiet down now> Come on folks, let's get started so we can all get back to our trees...," Elder Makin said, pounding the bottom of his pewter mug on the table. As the small crowd settled down, he paced back and forth in front of the room, his gnarled roots thumping loudly in the space. "Fairies of Bimblpea we have a problem. As you undoubtedly noticed, winter's still here, and spring is not! We are the first place that spring arrives every year, spreading out from our fields and forest to the rest of the land. In all my hundred and seventy-five years, Titania, Queen of Spring & Summer, has never been late. This delay is unnatural, and I fear she has been kidnapped, or worse!"

"She's a Fairy Queen—who could possibly have kidnapped her?" A voice shouted from the crowd.

I nodded at the very sensible question. Titania was quite powerful.

Elder Makin paused, considering. "It's not happened in my lifetime, but Palu the Goblin King has tried before. The stories say he managed to keep her for half a year. Maybe he's decided to try again? Or perhaps Oberon the Fairy King has imprisoned her? They are frequently at odds."

I knew Titania well, as did Hollybell and Lillipuff. "Do you remember that time when she and Oberon had that spectacular fight in the middle of the dancing glade?" I whispered to Hollybell.

Hollybell giggled. "I was so scared at the time, but then Titania came back to the bower and had a good laugh about it. I remember she was so merry about having pulled such a good prank, and the Elders were so careful around them for weeks."

"Oberon played his part well in that one too. Titania was so pleased," Lillipuff whispered quietly. I smiled at the memory—Titania had the most beautiful laugh, and she was frequently merry when we were all together.

We sighed in unison. As her ladies in waiting, we dined with her frequently and attended her throughout the spring and summer. By her own account, Titania and Oberon had a wonderful relationship, only infrequently marred by marital squabbling. They were quite in love, and while she was diligent in doing her duty to bring spring and summer to the world, she hated being parted from him. Keeping her against her will? It seemed unthinkable. Being kidnapped by a Goblin though or something as horrible ...

"I hope she's ok," I whispered to Lillipuff, who was sitting next to me.

Lillipuff nodded in agreement, listening to Elder Makin as he continued.

"People of Bimblpea—as the first recipient of spring, the nearby communities have come to us, asking us to help. They want us to put together a group to go and find Queen Titania and rescue her from her awful fate. If she does not return soon, we will all starve or freeze to death," Elder Makin said dramatically.

I flittered up out of my seat, my wings humming nervously. "Elder Makin, Queen Titania is only two weeks late, do you really think we need to send out a search party?" I felt all eyes swivel to me.

"Hmm. Is that young... Violet... I believe?" he replied, eyes boring into me above the crowd. "What would you have us tell the families who are running out of food because the flowers cannot get through the snow?"

"Elder Makin, very well, I agree, we should send someone to look for Queen Titania, but we should not malign Oberon in the process. It is not wise to speak ill of a King, and particularly not our Queen's consort," I said in a moderate tone. I saw nods of agreement in the crowd, and even the Elder paused at that.

"That is intelligently said," replied Elder Bodkin, one of the other council members. "We do not know what has happened. Given that you know more of Queen Titania than many of us, perhaps you should go and find her? See what is keeping her?" he inquired, thoughtfully.

"Ah. Um..." I stammered and looked down in panic. This was not where I intended this conversation to go. The idea of being out in the bitter cold, where wings could freeze and break off and flower petals would wither and die, frightened me. But Queen Titania was out there somewhere too, and she might need our help. The two ideas warred inside of me until my purple hands trembled.

"I don't want to, but someone needs to go," I replied as fear squeezed my chest. I looked back to the elders on the stage. "I will search and see what has become of our Queen." I was surprised when Lillipuff popped up out of her seat. "I shall go with her. We do not know how perilous the journey may be, and no one should go alone."

Hollybell stood as well. "I too will go on this journey. Since Spring has not appeared, we shall go look for her." Several of the fairies flew up in protest shouting, "Who will make the sugarplum treats and the tokens to leave for the children?"

This was Hollybell's area of expertise, and she looked at them pointedly. "If there are no flowers, then there is no nectar to make the treats from. Better that I help usher Spring back."

I chuckled under my breath. Hollybell did not suffer fools.

Lillipuff looked around. "We must leave in the morning. As such we have preparations to make. Elders, since this has been decided, I suggest we adjourn."

Elder Bodkin nodded in agreement and banged his gavel on the podium. "Ladies, we wish you luck and swift return on your quest."

Although fear still squeezed my chest, I was gratified that my friends chose to join me. Journeying into the unknown was not a task for the faint of heart.

Lillipuff, Hollybell and I adjourned to the sugarplum bakery since it was the nearest to the meeting hall. Hollybell closed the door behind us and began bringing out her amazing sugarplums, candied flowers and other delightful treats. She always had snacks. Lillipuff prepared tea while I bustled about laying out plates and napkins.

"Tomorrow we should leave early. I'll pack up food for us to take with us. Goodness knows I have plenty of leftover sugarplums from the midwinter celebrations, and they'll go to waste if I'm not here," Hollybell said.

My stomach was still in knots at the idea of leaving. "How can you be so calm?" I asked, admiring the older green fairy's demeanor.

"Oh Violet, once you've hit your first hundred-year mark you learn that nothing is ever as dire as it seems. I'm sure that there is a perfectly logical explanation as to why the Queen hasn't returned, and we will find out what it is. Now sit down and have a sugarplum. You'll need to go back to your tree soon and pack— bring your warmest gear."

Lillipuff poured the tea then sat, adjusting her delicate wings as she sipped daintily.

My wings shivered a little with fear. "We don't know what's out there or what we'll find. Titania told me a lot of stories, but..."

"We certainly have to be careful. I... I can bring my father's blackthorn dagger... It's the one he used in the goblin wars..." Lillipuff volunteered.

"Do you even know how to use it?" Hollybell asked, eyes wide.

"Well, my pa taught me a few things ..." she replied, picking nervously at the edge of a sugarplum.

"I... I can bring my blackthorn staff," I said. "It's not really intended as a weapon ... but it's sturdy at least..."

"Where do you think we should start looking?" Lillipuff asked.

"Queen Titania told me one time that the entrance to Oberon's kingdom is not far. She showed me a token once that would open the door. She used to tell me a lot of stories about his kingdom. I think the best place to start is there—where we know she was supposed to be." I bit my lip, thinking. "We'll also need some cheese."

Lillipuff got very excited, and her wings started buzzing. "I love cheese! Oh it's so tasty!"

"No!" Hollybell and I both said at the same time. "You know what it does to fairies."

"But... you just said we needed some..." she replied, crestfallen.

"According to what Titania has told me, we need to bring some cheese. It's not for us though." I said, giving Lillipuff a stern look. "Stay out of the cheese!"

Hollybell stared off into the distance for a moment. "I know where to get some goat cheese I think. There's a child at the edge of the village whose parents make it. I can trade for it. Will that do?" she asked quizzically. "Also, this is a lot of supplies, we can't fly with this much."

"We can't fly anyway. It's too cold, and our wings are brittle," Lillipuff replied, still pouting.

"Violet, will you be able to bring the wagon with you?" Hollybell asked.

"Will a wagon work in this snow...?" I questioned.

"This is much more complicated than I thought it would be," Lillipuff huffed.

"I know—a toboggan!" Hollybell exclaimed.

"And we'll need a carriage mouse to help pull everything," I replied, the pieces falling into place.

"It sounds like we have a plan," Hollybell replied, and she sparkled in anticipation. I wondered if it was enough of a plan.

The next day, watery sunlight filtered through clouds, creating illusive rainbows but providing very little warmth. I had spent the evening getting my cozy little house ready for an extended absence, retrieving Titania's token from her chambers, and piling supplies on our toboggan. I met Hollybell and Lillipuff at the candy shop. It was close to mid-morning by the time everything was ready, and several of the fairies had come by to wish us luck.

"Watch out for hawks!" one townsfairy shouted as we pulled out into the street. I shivered. It wasn't an idle warning—the hawks, dangerous unto themselves, had been allies of the Goblin king since the goblin wars.

Our carriage mouse, Francis was a stoic, determined little rodent. He didn't speak much, but then again only the dancing mice did that. This was a task he was born into. He waited patiently while we hitched the toboggan and loaded all the supplies.

Lillipuff said, "Ok ladies, we have a job to do. Violet, lead on."

"Um. Where are we going?" Hollybell asked. "Do you know?"

I took a deep breath and focused on the job at hand. The cold was brutal, and I had my wings tucked in snugly against my back, constrained by my warm cloak of woven moss. "Follow the glitter pebble path for a day and a night, and then we'll find the marker stone. There's another path there—it's easy to see in the summer, but I'm not sure how visible it will be with all this snow."

"I guess we'll find out," Hollybell said cheerfully.

Lillipuff nodded, giving the mouse's bridle a gentle tap to get him moving. "Let's get going."

The trek to the marker stone proved to be a two-day journey—entirely due to the heavy snow that slowed us down and obscured the path. I was pleased that we found it at all. Under the trees, the snow was lighter and less packed, but we still had to struggle through, and occasionally, an ominous shadow from above crossed our path. Francis pulled the toboggan without fail, but every time a shadow flew overhead, he paused, and as the night got colder, it became harder and harder to pull. We finally stopped in the shelter of a large tree root and built a small fairy fire to warm ourselves and Francis. We were fortunate that the hawks moving above hadn't seen us. When sunlight tickled the air, we began our trek again. After three days we reached the entrance of The Cave.

Oberon was not the king of the underworld, but rather the king of the dark fairies, and they preferred to live in caves, and dark places under the earth. Titania joined her king for half the year in his kingdom, ruling with him until the last day of winter, when she returned to her own people. I always thought this strange, since Oberon never joined her in her kingdom, but I had never been bold enough to inquire.

Once we got to what I thought was the proper cave, I said, "In her many stories, Titania told how to find the entrance. She said that it looked like nothing more than a small overhang, protected from the snow, but with a massive tree on either side," I mused. "This certainly seems to fit her description. She said the way to know for sure was that, near the top of the overhang where the stone met, there would be a small carving of spring flowers, hidden unless you looked at it from a certain angle."

"Let's search around and see if we can find it. It will match

Titania's royal seal."

We began searching, and a few minutes later Lillipuff exclaimed, "Here it is!" She pointed out a carving on the stone wall, no bigger than my hand, of a bouquet of spring flowers.

"This must be it!" I said, excitement making my wings hum under my cloak. "Okay, once we enter, if we get separated, look for those carved symbols and follow them back," I said quietly. "We won't be able to take Francis with us, but he should be fine here." Not that I thought there was any chance we'd be able to get Francis to enter the cave. He was already staring at it nervously. "We'll leave him tethered with food and water—if the worst happens, he'll gnaw through the tether." I looked at my two friends, trying to keep the look of worry off my face.

Lillipuff looked around the small cave and nodded. "Before we venture into the dark realm we should probably eat something. Never know what we're going to find, but it's always better to face challenges on a full stomach."

I nodded. "That's an excellent idea." I rummaged through the bags looking for the sugarplums. "What do you think happened to her?" I asked out of the blue.

"I'm worried about our queen," Hollybell murmured.

"Do you think maybe the Goblin king is involved?" Lillipuff asked.

"Why would the Goblin king kidnap her again?" Hollybell replied, looking up from unhitching Francis.

Everyone knew the story of how Oberon was quite angry and stole the Goblin King's children away in revenge. Setting an armful of firewood down as she cleared a space for the fire, Lillipuff replied, "Oberon certainly made his point the last time."

"I heard he also sealed all the entrances to the Goblin King's realm and loosed his power within, driving the adult goblins mad with noises in the dark. There were things that went bump in the night that could touch them, but that they could not affect," I said, shuddering.

Silence as we all considered what a truly angry Goblin king might do to any fairy in revenge. By the time full dark arrived, we had a fire going, and Lillipuff had a sugarplum stew simmering. Francis was happily munching on a pile of acorns. We settled in, the cave providing a cozy backdrop. But I must confess, I did not sleep well.

In the morning the snow was coming down hard. We added more acorns to Francis's pile, and I held the token of safe passage up to Queen Titania symbol. The stone melted away as if it had never existed. Lillipuff and Hollybell stood, mouths agape looking at the shimmering curtain. "This is how she described it, so I guess we're in the right place?" I said nervously, putting the token back in my pouch.

I stepped through, drawing them in after me. We entered a grey and desolate landscape. A flat plane of sand stretched before us, seemingly never ending. It was all grey. The sky was grey, the sand was grey, and there were no markers to get our bearings. Every ounce of color seemed to be eaten up by the never ending grey. I turned to my friends, and I stared, horrified. The beautiful colors of their cloaks, wings and skin were being drained from them. Our own colors seemed muted, slowly turning from our vibrant hues to subdued shades, as if the color was leeching out of us. I quickly realized the danger. "We have to do this and get out of here quickly. If we lose our color, we will become part of the landscape and never be able to leave!" I said, panic causing my wings to buzz under my cloak.

"Look! There's her next marker!" I shouted, crossing the sand to the wide, flat rock with Titania's carved symbol in it. Hollybell and Lillipuff followed me, looking around in a panic. I searched the horizon, there was nothing there. "No matter what you hear or see, do not stray further than three or four steps from Titania's marker my dear friends. And do not touch the water." I said, as I tried to remember what Titania had told me about the guardian here.

They looked confused at that. "Violet, are you all right? There is no water, anywhere," Hollybell said, gesturing to the dry plains.

"You'll see." I took three strides away from the marker and held up Queen Titania's token. "I hope this works!" I remember her telling me this story because I thought the name was funny, but it wasn't funny now.

"Vodník, I have need of you!" I called loudly and firmly three times. Without warning a river appeared rising out of the sand like tidal waters rushing in at high tide. I jumped back before the waters could touch me for in their touch lay forgetfulness. I turned to warn Lillipuff and Hollybell, but they had already stepped back. Strangely they were peering in my direction as if looking through a dense fog.

"Who roused me from my slumber?" I heard a powerful, watery voice call out. I turned around, and there he was. Vodník was an ancient water sprite. He was not friendly, but he could be convinced to be talkative, if offered the correct incentive. As he appeared, rising from the water, I fished the packet of goat cheese out, unwrapped it, and bowed. "A gift for you sir, in the hopes that you can answer a question or two for us."

He was quite a bit taller than me, a naked, potbellied man-figure, wearing a belt of reeds and water weed. Bits of algae clung to his mottled skin, giving him a sickly appearance, and the smell of rotted fish clung to him. He sniffed the air, and stepped out of the water, reaching out for the cheese. I stood quietly while he took in the aroma and broke off a small crumble and popped it into his mouth.

"Mmm. Very good." His low voice rumbled, sounding like water over rocks as he looked over our trio. "I cannot take you across without a token," he said, his voice making it a question of our intent rather than a statement.

"We have no wish to cross at this time. Can you answer a question for us? Is Queen Titania still in Oberon's kingdom?" I inquired, watching him closely.

"No. She left some time ago, she and Oberon both. Erick and I have been keeping things protected while they're gone."

I felt my jaw hanging open in surprise and snapped my mouth shut. I had not expected so complete an answer. "Ah—did she give any indication where she was going or when she'd be back?"

Vodník stared off into the distance, still chewing on the small pieces of goat cheese. "This is very good cheese," he said, after a moment. I waited in silence to see if he would continue. Another few moments passed as he stared across the river. Into the deepening silence he said, "Oberon said they were going to... hold on, I wrote this down," He fished about in the water weeds around his waist, and I realized it was actually a belt with pouches. "Ah, here we are," he peered at a scrap of parchment. "They are somewhere called Vac Asion. It sounded like a long journey, but I don't know where it is."

I shook my head. "I also have not heard of this. Where is this land?"

Vodník contemplated my question, the silence growing longer and more uncomfortable. He had no answers for me. I could see Hollybell and Lillipuff from the corner of my eye. Their colors were almost gone!

"I thank you Vodník," I said hurriedly. "I must get back to my friends."

Vodník picked off another bite of cheese. "And I must get back to my charges. Thank you for the cheese."

I quickly stepped back to Titania's marker, watching as he sank down and the water swiftly receded. Hollybell and Lillipuff looked startled as I grabbed their hands.

"How did you do that?" Hollybell demanded. "What did the two of you say to each other?"

I pulled them both frantically back towards the marker that held the cave entrance. "Come on! We have to get out of here before our colors fade!" I said, dragging them behind me.

"Why didn't you take us with you?" Lillipuff demanded, digging in her heels.

"What do you mean, where did I go? I was standing right there the whole time talking to Vodník. Hollybell shook her head confused.

"You left us in this place with no explanation and no warning. One minute you gestured us through a door to the dark kingdom, the next you vanished into thin air."

"You were gone. Just... gone." Lillipuff shook her head.

"I was standing right there the whole time. I could see both of you while I spoke to Vodník." I replied.

"Vodník was here?!" Hollybell said, looking around skeptically.

"Yes—I used Queen Titania's token to call him, and thankfully he came. I wasn't sure he would. It was very unsettling. He did like your cheese though, Hollybell, so I'm glad we brought it. Now come on! We must get out of here. Questions later!" I said, resorting to pushing them from behind to propel them forward. "Look at your hands, your color is almost gone!"

"Oh, this place is so peaceful and relaxing," I heard Lillipuff say, suddenly twirling around in a circle. "I think I'll just sit down and take a little nap."

Panic set in truly at that moment. "Hollybell—focus. We must get out of here NOW. Help me with Lillipuff, or we'll all succumb to the grey."

Hollybell shook her head. "It's a good thing we've known each other for years, or I'd be questioning your sanity about now."

"I swear it's all true. He said that... Never mind. We have to go. Lillipuff, don't you want to check on Francis?" I asked, trying to grab her attention again, as I hauled her up from the sand. Lillipuff rolled her eyes but followed me back to the portal stone.

"I'm sure he's fine," she said, flouncing in annoyance. "It's so nice here..." she started to wander off again, and I grabbed her arm and spun her around to the portal, shoving her through.

I breathed a sigh of relief when we were all back in the cave. Our color started to return almost immediately, and I saw Lillipuff give herself a little shake, as if coming out of a trance. Hollybell shook her head, looking around in confusion.

"What is going on?" Hollybell demanded.

"Fair question," I replied. The snow was still coming down thickly outside the overhang. "Let's get a fire going, and I'll tell you everything that happened from my perspective."

As the fire crackled, I told them everything I had seen, and everything Vodník had said, and how they had lost almost all their color before we got back. "So, they've traveled to a land called, Vac Asion?" Hollybell asked after she'd listened to all that I had to say.

"That's what Vodník said," I replied with a helpless shrug.

"I've read a lot, and looked at a lot of maps in Titania's library. There's no reference to a place called Vac Asion anywhere. I'm certain of it." Hollybell stared into the fire morosely.

"What do you mean?" Lillipuff wailed. "We don't know where she is or how to find her?" she sniffled. The grey seemed to have affected her more than the rest of us, and she was still not quite back to full vibrancy. "We're lost, it's cold, it's still snowing, and I'm scared. I want to go home!" she wailed again, bursting into tears.

Hollybell put a comforting arm around Lillipuff and looked across the fire to me. "She's right. We don't know where to go next. We really should go home."

It was logical, we should go home, but I wasn't quite ready to give up yet. "We can try one more thing. Isn't there a village of ice fairies around here somewhere?"

Hollybell nodded, "It's just across the plain that starts on the other side of that hill," she replied, gesturing towards the east. "But it's exposed plains almost the whole way."

"I think we should go there. At least until we figure out what we should do."

"It is closer than going home, and it would give us a chance to get more supplies at least," Hollybell said reasonably. "But that open plain—we'll be exposed to the hawks the entire way."

Lillipuff shuddered, no doubt thinking about what the Goblin King would do to us if we were caught.

"We'll be careful," I promised. "I feel like we should keep looking. At least a bit longer. Maybe they'll have some ideas."

By morning the snow had stopped, and the world was blanketed in stillness. Every surface glittered like diamonds, and I had to shield my eyes when I stepped out of the cave entrance. "Oooh pretty!" Lillipuff squealed behind her.

Hollybell stuck her head out of the cave and looked around. "Bundle up tight today ladies, it's beautiful, but it will be colder than an ice fairy's foot once the breeze starts up!"

I nodded in agreement. The three of us were spring fairies and not built for this type of weather. Francis was eager to get out, and once he was harnessed, we flew across the new snow, towards the break in the hills, leaving little puffs flying up in our wake. Traveling through the forest this way was bizarre. I was used to seeing green grass and flowers, and new wild strawberries, not this endless blanket of white, and the hushed tones of a wilderness still asleep. It wasn't as scary as the grey domain we had just escaped from, but it was unnerving. We pushed onward, even little, determined Francis, though I could see he was weakening with every step. The cold was taking a toll on him too. Every once in a while, through the branches above us, we'd see the dreaded shadow of a hawk, circling, the shadow sending a shiver of fear down our spines. In late afternoon, we reached the edge of the forest and stopped, staring across the vast expanse of flat, white open land, where we could just see the river on the far side. It was intimidating, how exposed everything was.

Lillipuff saw it and hid her face with her hands. "We'll never be able to get across that safely. That hawk has been following us the entire way, and we'd be totally at his mercy!" As if to punctuate her point, we heard the piercing call of a hawk far above us.

I shivered, looking around. "We must though." I peered more closely at the ground beneath our feet, here at the forest edge, and then kicked the snow away until I could see it clearly. "What if..." I began digging down into the dirt, trying to get my fingers under the edge of the thick turf. With much pulling and heaving, I was able to get a section of mossy turf to come loose. "What if we use this to cover the toboggan and we hide underneath it? Then the Hawk wouldn't be able to see us."

I could see Hollybell running through the possibilities in her head, weighing out the pros and cons. After a moment she said, "I think it could work. We can even cover up some of Francis too, though of course he needs to be able to see where he's going. We'll have to move slowly though."

Nodding, I set to pulling up more sections of turf, while Hollybell and Lillipuff arranged them over the toboggan and covered them back with snow, until it looked like an overly large tuft of bush. "Well done! There's no way a hawk will be able to spot us now, so long as we don't move too fast."

Francis was none too pleased with his blanket of moss and snow but only grumbled a bit. We loaded ourselves in hiding under the disguising blanket and set off, ever so slowly, across the plain. Every time the shadow of the hawk crossed our path, Francis froze, and we waited nerve wracking moments to see if it had spotted us. We were halfway to the river when the small, enclosed space of the moss covered toboggan was flooded with the overwhelming scent of cinnamon. My eyes began to water profusely, and Hollybell whispered, "Who did that!"

I shook my head, it wasn't me. We both looked to Lillipuff who had turned bright orange with embarrassment. Then we heard a small 'toot' and there was another engulfing wave of Cinnamon.

"I'm so sorry!" she said frantically. "I can't control it."

Dawning horror washed across my face. "Did you eat some of the cheese?!"

"I couldn't help myself! I love cheese! It was only a small piece," she wailed, her voice becoming louder.

"And seriously, NOW is when you decided to do it?"

"Shh!" Hollybell gestured frantically. "He'll hear us!"

We all froze, waiting, hoping he would pass us by. He didn't. He landed in the snow next to us, peering down at the oddly shaped tuft that was our toboggan, studying it with his beady eyes. His beak was just getting ready to nip at the top of the tuft, when something distracted him, and he launched himself into the air.

I let out the breath I'd been holding, shivering in fear. That had been far too close.

We began moving slowly across the plain again. Just as we reached the edge of the frozen river, there was another soft 'toot'. The smell was overpowering in the confined space, and almost immediately the shadow of the hawk was upon us again. We only had to get across the river, and we could hide at the edge of the forest there, but we still had to navigate the ice.

Francis moved ever so slowly out onto the frozen river, cowering every time the hawk came near. Lillipuff let out another toot.

"Give me your dagger," I said, scowling, trying not to inhale the overpowering scent.

"Never again. I will never eat cheese again," she whispered in frantic promises.

"Dagger, now. I need to create a distraction for that hawk," I replied, wanting to strangle her. She handed it to me, and I leaned out, stabbing into the ice, creating a small hole. Frigid water spurted out, drenching us, but as we moved away, it continued to bubble up onto the ice. The hawk honed in on the burbling water and landed, eyeing it suspiciously, giving us enough time to get to the riverbank and hide under the first set of tree-roots we could find.

We huddled close, watching as the hawk continued to circle the open plain, further and further away. We had made it. When we could no longer see him, I gave a sigh of relief and collapsed. Suddenly, a fit of the giggles overtook me.

"Lillipuff, what were you thinking?" I hiccuped out, the hilarity of the situation hitting me. "We were almost eaten by a hawk because you tooted!"

Hollybell looked at me, then at Lillipuff and chuckled, then guffawed, and then we were all rolling on the ground laughing until we were gasping for breath.

"You looked so funny, turning bright orange and wondering if you could blame it on one of us," I chortled, poking Lillipuff in the ribs.

She laughed weakly, "I just can't help it around cheese—you know that. It's SO good. I didn't think a little taste would hurt."

Still snickering, Hollybell stuck her head out of our hiding place. "I think the village is just over there a little further. We should try and get there before we freeze or get sick with all this wet clothing."

The thought of moving again was exhausting, I just wanted to curl up into a little ball and go to sleep, but I forced myself upright, wavering on my feet. "Maybe they'll have some warm food they'll share with us..."

"Come on you two, let's hide the toboggan here. I don't think Francis can pull it any further in any case. He's exhausted too," Hollybell said, rousting us to help her. We unhitched Francis and covered the toboggan with the snowy moss, concealing it from prying eyes.

It was a miserable hike through the snow, and we were all weak from hunger and cold. When we reached the settlement, I was ready to collapse. I could see the strain on Hollybell and Lillipuff's faces as well. The town was celebrating, with tinsel and ice sculptures and music at every corner. People stared as we entered the main street—we were out of place here. I imagine we looked awful, bedraggled, wrapped in moss, heads hanging. My feet wouldn't move any further, and I stood swaying in the middle of the street uncertain of where to go.

"Are you okay? Do you need help?" An ice fairy approached us cautiously, his blue body and white clothing sparkling in the frosty air.

"Food. We need food, and warmth." I thought I had said it, but it was Hollybell, when I didn't respond.

The fairy nodded. "This way, it's just around the corner. Can you make it that far?"

My feet followed him, though my voice didn't respond. He went slowly, making sure we kept up, and to my relief, he wasn't exaggerating—there was a tavern just around the corner. A stable fairy took Francis's lead from me and promised to warm him up and feed him.

A blessed rush of warmth engulfed us as we entered, and the blue fairy settled the three of us on a bench with a table to ourselves.

I began shedding moss immediately, leaving it in a pile at my feet. The warmth helped, and I looked around. It was a prosperous looking tavern, with several fairies seated at the bar and at tables throughout. I thought it odd that everyone looked as exhausted as I felt. The blue fairy returned with a tray full of things to eat, and I could see he was sweating profusely. He looked at us, surprised, as he set the food down.

"Spring and summer fairies? Here? No wonder you looked so awful. The cold is no place for your kind." He handed us mugs of a steaming drink. "Mulled wine to warm you. I brought some food as well. Why are the three of you all the way here?" he asked with puzzlement.

I took a long sip of the hot wine, and I saw Hollybell and Lillipuff do so as well, warming their fingers on the mugs. "You haven't by chance seen our queen here?"

He slid onto a bench opposite us, "I'm Frig by the way."

"Oh dear, how rude of me. My mind isn't working very well at the moment. Thank you so much for helping us, Frig. This is Hollybell and Lillipuff," I replied, gesturing to my companions. "We've had quite the trip to get here."

He nodded a polite round of greetings. "Yes, Queen Titania is here, she's presiding over the winter revels with King Oberon this year."

I felt something loosen in my chest, and Hollybell sighed with relief. "We must speak with her immediately!" Lillipuff said. "It's quite urgent."

"Wait, she's here? How long has she been here?" I asked our new friend.

He looked uneasy at the question, glancing around to see who might overhear. "She's been here for about a month, along with the king."

Hollybell looked at me, then at him. "I thought she was supposed to be in some place called Vac Asion. Have you heard of it?"

Frig shook his head. "I can't say that I have."

I shrugged. "Perhaps Vodník had it wrong? In any case it doesn't matter, she's here. We need to see her right away."

Frig looked us over, as if considering his next words, and then he smiled broadly. "I think you will want to eat, and bathe before you approach the king and queen," he replied, looking around the room. I looked at Hollybell and Lillipuff, and noted the bedraggled hair, the mud-stained clothing, the twigs poking out at odd angles and imagined that I must look at least as comical. Hollybell looked at me and burst out in giggles. "Oh, Violet, you have bits of acorn and twigs all over you, and Lillipuff your hair is a right mess," she said giggling.

Smiling wryly, I replied, "That is an excellent idea. Although we have come a long way, and it is urgent that we see Queen Titania as soon as possible."

Frig nodded. "Stay here and eat your food, I will arrange it with the innkeeper, and then I must be on my way before I melt. Only visitors stay here. It's much too warm for us ice fae."

"Oh, what luck that we found someone so helpful," Hollybell said, taking another sip of her mulled wine.

"And handsome!" Lillipuff replied with a twinkle in her eye. I was pleased to see some of the glimmer coming back into her face, and her color was starting to return to her usual cheerful yellow. Frig spoke with the fairy at the bar for a long few moments, gesturing back to the three of us. The barkeep looked over and nodded as Frig continued talking. The fairy behind the bar passed him some tokens and Frig rejoined us. "Ladies, I've secured you rooms, and a turn at the bathhouse here. These are your tokens. The innkeeper will see that your cloaks are cleaned as well. I'll be back in the morning to collect you."

Lillipuff giggled, "Thank you so much! You've been so kind to us," she said, smiling up at him and batting her eyelashes.

Frig's smile gleamed, and his wings sparkled a bit brighter. "I'm happy to help! I look forward to seeing you tomorrow."

The bathhouse was like nothing we had ever experienced before. Once we finished our food and mulled wine, and we had thawed out enough to expand our wings again, stiff with disuse, a server came and showed us where our rooms were and how to access the bathhouse. It was luxurious. A wall of damp, warm air wafted out the open door, smelling like spring and summer wrapped into one. Pools of water for soaking and bathing were carved into tiers in the floors, with channels built in to take the dirty water away. The floors were warm to walk on, though no heat source was visible. Gradually, after washing, and soaking in the warm waters, I felt the cold seep out of my bones and could see the glimmer start to come back to my purple wingtips. Once I was warm, and Hollybell and Lillipuff were relaxing in soaking tubs nearby, I asked, "Do you think it strange that Frig seems so accommodating? He doesn't know us after all."

"Violet, don't be so suspicious," Lillipuff replied, stretching luxuriously in the warm water. "Clearly he's a helpful soul who saw that we were in need."

Hollybell snorted, inhaled some water, and began coughing, laughing all the while. "Lillipuff, you are perhaps the naivest fairy I've ever met. However, I didn't sense any ill-intent from the young man. And even if there is ill-intent to come, right now I'm going to enjoy my hot soak."

"Well, I don't like to be suspicious, but I think we should keep our heads about us. He mentioned something about the queen celebrating the winter revels with Oberon, but Vodník said she had left to a faraway land. And the winter revels should long since be over. Something's going on."

I sat back in the warm water trying to relax, trying to puzzle out what might be delaying our queen. The fairies at home were depending on us, and Spring was now more than a month overdue.

The next morning, we met in the common room for a hearty breakfast of berries and nectar. Hollybell and Lillipuff were looking much better, and I could see their glimmer returning. It wasn't full yet, but light sparkled off their wings, and their colors were returning to their normal, vibrant shades. A full night's rest in the warm, cozy inn had done wonders. Frig returned, just as promised, and looked us up and down, smiling. "Ah, my Spring and Summer cousins, you are looking much restored! It broke my heart to see you so dull and downtrodden yesterday. Now let us see if we can get you to your queen! It is quite cold out again today, so bundle up!"

As promised, the Innkeeper had sent our cloaks out to be cleaned, and they were returned to us, smelling much better, if stained and travelworn. We wrapped them carefully around our wings and followed Frig into the snow. He led us, along with a flood of other fairies, to the festival grounds on the outskirts of town. We passed snow sculptures, fairies gliding across a frozen pond to music, booths of food both hot and cold, a field for sporting competitions, and finally a grandstand where King Oberon and his court sat, presiding over it all. Queen Titania sat by his side, bundled in the warmest of colorful cloaks, smiling and laughing and waving at the crowds.

A sigh of relief escaped my lips. "She's okay!" My wings fluttered and buzzed in excitement, even held down by my cloak.

I waved frantically at her, trying to get her attention, mentally begging her to look our way, and Hollybell and Lilipuff did the same. My feet flew across the fairgrounds toward her, dodging celebrants, and participants alike. As we approached the grandstand at some speed, the king's guards intercepted us, blocking our way.

"Please, we must speak to the queen! We come with news of her kingdom," I shouted, straining to see past the two tall ice fairies that blocked our path.

"The queen is busy and does not wish to be disturbed," the ice fairy said coldly.

"Queen Titania!" I shouted. "Please! We need to speak with you!"

"Quiet!" the guard said rudely. "She does not wish to be disturbed. You may submit your petition to be heard during the audience session. The next one is next month."

Hollybell gasped beside me. "This cannot wait for a month! We have news of the kingdom! Lives depend on us speaking to her."

"Queen Titania! I shouted again, waving my arms frantically, trying to draw her attention. The queen did not see me, but King Oberon did, and I saw him draw Titania's attention to him, blocking me from her sight. I gasped, and a chill of fear went through my wings. Why didn't the king want her to notice us?

'If you do not cease making a scene, we will be forced to detain you in the palace dungeon," the guard said as Hollybell continued arguing.

I grabbed her hand and gave it a squeeze so that she turned to look at me, and I said to the guard, "Thank you for your time. We will put in a petition as you suggested," I said as I pulled Hollybell away back towards Frig and Lillipuff.

"What is going on?" I demanded of Frig.

He looked around, and then led us off from the crowd. "Oh good. You saw it. I didn't know how to explain it to you. I don't know what's going on, but since I've never met the queen, I wasn't sure if this was normal. She shouldn't be here. It's long past the time where we are all supposed to be resting for the spring. I love the winter revels, but they've gone on much too long. It's starting to take a toll; everyone's exhausted, and we're just putting on a show. No one is having any fun."

"Why didn't you say something then?" I demanded.

"I couldn't. Because things are not right here, and I don't know who to trust. It's very hard to tell friend from foe, and I don't know who might have reported on me. Also, I needed time to think," Frig replied.

He took a deep breath,."When I saw the three of you in the street yesterday, I was hoping you had a solution."

"Is our queen being held?" I asked

"I don't know," he replied, frustrated.

"Is she bespelled?" Hollybell asked

"I don't know!" he replied, pulling on his hair.

"Well, what do we do now?" Lillipuff said with an annoyed little huff. "Clearly the guards aren't going to let us anywhere near her, and the King is keeping her too distracted to even notice us."

"You've got to get us in to see her," I said.

"What good would that do?" Frig asked. "Do you think she'll listen to you if you can talk to her personally?" Frig asked, glancing around, lowering his voice.

"We are her friends and her attendants. I cannot imagine she would deny us, should she know we are here," Hollybell said.

"Can you sneak us into the palace?" I asked. "Or somehow help us get to her?"

Frig thought for a moment. I could tell he was trying to decide how much to trust us. "My friend Icic attends the queen. I think I can convince her to help get you past the guards. If I do though, please, you have to convince her to leave. We love her, but seasons change for a reason!" The desperation and panic in Frig's voice did more to convince me than words ever could. The ice fairies were in the same plight as us but being tied to the king, they could not approach or convince the queen. It had to be members of her own court.

I nodded. "Get us to her, and we will do the rest," I replied, hoping I wasn't promising too much. Looking back over my shoulder, I tried to find the queen, but she was no longer in the grandstand. King Oberon stared at our colorful little group, making me uncomfortable. "I think we should go back to the inn and stay out of sight. I get the feeling that the King is not happy with our presence here."

Frig paled and quickly led the three of us back the way we had come.

That night, under cover of darkness and heavy cloaks to hide our glimmer, we followed Frig to the Royal Ice palace. He was wearing a blue and silver uniform that looked like that of the guards we had met earlier. We were fortunate that the moon had not yet risen. This place was unlike anything I had seen before—Titania did not have such a dwelling in the forest, preferring trees, meadows, and open sky. Here everything was made of cold, glistening ice, including the walls and doors. It would have been beautiful if my heart wasn't so heavy. Guards stood watch in the hallways, and servants moved about with bowed heads. It was frightening in its stark differences from our home.

"Once we get in the palace, follow behind me, and no matter what, don't say anything and don't let anyone see under your cloaks. All the queen's servants have been spelled to silence." He led us through the outer door, and down several hallways, until we came to a kitchen. There he flagged a woman down and whispered in her ear. "These are the friends I told you about. They must get to the queen tonight!" This was Icic I assumed.

The woman nodded, but didn't say a word, simply gestured for us to follow her. She picked up a tray bearing a variety of foods and handed it to me, then a pewter pitcher full of mead to Hollybell, and then laid out a napkin and towel on Lillipuff's arm. We had to be careful that our cloaks covered as much of us as possible. Once we were laden, she gestured again, and we followed her down a long corridor. It was nerve wracking trying to walk past the guards as if we belonged, but we managed, walking at a hurried pace. Finally Icic opened an ornate door to an even more ornate room.

A figure sat in the sitting area at the far end of the suite, staring into the fire. Icic took the tray and pitcher from us, and we rushed across the suite. "Titania!" I cried.

The figure rose, and turned to look at us, and we froze. It was not our queen, but rather King Oberon. "You three!" He shouted. "I thought that was you at the fairgrounds. What are you doing here, you'll ruin everything!"

"What have you done to Queen Titania! Why have you bespelled her? She's supposed to be back in the summerlands by now. Why are you keeping her here out of season!" I shouted back, trembling.

"You dare speak to your king that way!" King Oberon roared, and I could see the winter storm clouds gathered around his head. I took a step back, then another, and then I felt Hollybell and Lillipuff's hands on my shoulders. We couldn't back down now. All the fairies of Bimblpea were depending on us, and our friend the queen might be in danger.

"Give her back!" I said, spine stiffening. "You must give her back. We cannot survive without her."

"Oberon! What is the meaning of this?" I heard Titania's voice behind me, and turned to look at my queen. She looked at him, confused.

"My dear attendants, what are you doing awake at midwinter? You are all out of season. Oberon, why are they here, and why are you yelling at them?"

I glanced over at Oberon and back to Titania. "My Queen, it is not midwinter. We lack but a week to the first of May."

Titania looked at Oberon, "My darling, is what they are saying true? How did this come to be? I remember quite well, we are here to celebrate the midwinter revels?"

Oberon gazed at his queen with sad, adoring eyes, and then sighed. "My skylark of spring, when you prepared to leave for your kingdom at the appointed time, I thought to myself, 'Oh how I miss her when she is gone. I wish to keep her with me for just one more day.' And..." He looked down, ashamed. "...so I prepared a small spell, nothing big, that would convince you that it was the day before. And it worked beautifully. I got to spend another day with you..."

He sighed. "Then I cast it again. And I have cast it again every day since, not wanting to be out of your presence for even a moment."

Titania looked at him in shocked silence. Little sparks of lightning started running down the edges of her wings, and thunderclouds gathered at her brow. "You. Lied. To ME." It was a statement full of hurt, and anger and rage, and Oberon flinched under her glare.

"My darling, light of my life, I only thought—you were so tired, and upset by having to leave. I thought you could use a small vacation. It... admittedly did get out of hand."

I locked eyes with Hollybell as I realized. Vac Asion. Vacation. Hollybell realized just as I did and shook her head. Vacation.

"Oberon, of course I never want to leave you, but ruling over Spring and Summer is my duty! My people are suffering. As a ruler you know very well that you must do what is best for your subjects and not what is best for yourself."

The queen looked around and saw Icic standing quietly near the table. "You. You've served me here since I arrived. Why did you not tell me?"

Icic looked miserable and shook her head. "Why did no-one tell me?" The queen demanded.

Icic shook her head, looking even more miserable. "Answer me!" The Queen demanded.

Icic cried, little snowflakes falling from her eyes. "My Queen, Titania, she can't speak. She's been bespelled, as have all your servants," Lillipuff said sadly.

"Bespelled, you say?" Titania replied, and I could see color rising in her, all over again, all the shades of the rainbow playing across her skin. "Who would dare such a thing?"

"Your Majesty," Hollybell said deferentially. "We came here to find you and convince you to come back to your kingdom to resume your duties. We have not had time to investigate deeper plots. It is urgent that you return. That said—there are only two fairies powerful enough to bespell other fairies—you, and King Oberon."

Ignoring Oberon, she said to us, "I must needs have more of a conversation with my husband. Ladies, it is never pleasant to witness the squabbles of a married couple, and I will not subject you to it now. Please return in the morning, and we will leave immediately following the morning meal to set things to rights. Don't be late, or you will have to take the long way home. You have done me a great service this night, and we will speak more of it in days to come."

We dropped hurried curtsies to her and to the king and scurried out of the room, closing the door behind us.

"Oberon!" We heard her shout, and the walls of the palace trembled. The Queen of Spring and Summer had at her power the anger of storms as well as the joy of the bumble bee. "It is true then that you have been deceiving me. Keeping me here long past the time I should be performing my duties!" Lightning flashed in the chamber, visible even through the opaque ice walls.

"Titania, my dearest, I was only trying to help. You looked so tired, and I thought the winter revels would help restore some of that joyous feeling between us. It's been a very long time since we've been able to relax."

"And you thought the best way to do that was to lie to me and keep me from my duties?" she spat.

"It... may not... have been the... correct approach. But you have had a month of being able to attend festivals, and fetes, and no-one to trouble you with the worries of a kingdom. It was intended as a gift. But perhaps I did allow it to go on a bit too long," he said, trying to curb her anger.

"You bespelled the servants so they couldn't talk to me! And lied about the date. May Day is less than a week away, and my kingdom is in shambles!" she shouted. "I demand you lift the spell on the servers immediately. How wicked of you to mute them, how villainous of you to lie to me, your wife!"

Oberon's voice was quiet and harder to hear as we got further from the room. "My dearest, I am sorry that my plan for frivolity has gone awry and that you are displeased," he said earnestly. "Let us set things to rights between us and then set things to rights in your kingdom."

Icic hiccuped behind us, and a soft sound came out. She looked shocked, and a swirl of snowflakes fell from her eyes. "The spell... the spell is gone! I can talk again!" She whispered and then burst into full tears, babbling. "Thank you so much for helping. I haven't been able to speak to my wife in weeks, and I thought I would burst! I must go see her. She will be so relieved."

We followed Icic out of the castle, listening to her babble all the way, as she rejoiced in the return of her voice.

Frig was outside and looked both relieved and worried to see us. We filled him in as we walked back to the inn. "Spring will return tomorrow? We don't have to keep up the charade of the winter revels any longer? Icic has her voice back too!" He sounded so relieved that he couldn't contain himself. "Thank you all so much!"

I was still feeling nervous and out of sorts, and as we made our way back to the inn, I could see thunderclouds moving in surrounding the castle. "I think Titania is not yet done with her conversation with Oberon. Frig, Icic, I suggest that you warn as many people as possible to get indoors and stay indoors. There will be a storm tonight the likes of which you have never seen." I pointed back to the clouds surrounding the castle, and Frig's pale skin paled further.

"You can find your way from here?" he inquired.

We nodded and watched him sprint for the center of town. A few minutes later a bell began ringing wildly, and shortly thereafter we saw streams of ice fairies coming into town, some running, some propelling themselves on long flat boards attached to their feet, and a few flying. Hurrying to the inn, we saw the innkeeper boarding up the windows and stacking wood and kindling next to the front door for easy access. "Ladies, best get inside quickly. The storm's almost here."

It raged that night, and the guests at the inn huddled in the main room drinking mulled wine long after they would normally have gone to bed. Well after midnight, we retired to our rooms to try and sleep, hoping that we'd be able to get back to the castle in the morning. Sometime in the night, the king and queen's anger must have resolved itself. The morning dawned clear, and the temperature was rising, causing the snow to melt off quickly, sending rivulets of water down the mountain.

Frig joined us at the inn and then accompanied us back to the castle in the morning, leading Francis behind him. "Lillipuff, you can't imagine how happy Icic's wife was when she returned home, even with the storm blowing in. I checked in on them before returning home. She was radiant."

Lillipuff giggled and smiled, putting her arm through his, a glimmer sending sparks from her wings. "I'm so glad! And I'm glad you came to see us off. I hope we can see you again."

I smiled, listening to them. I didn't think Frig could tell, but Lillipuff was clearly enamored of him.

"Come on you two—the queen said that if we weren't there in time, we'd have to take the long way home, and I for one have no desire to traipse back," Hollybell called over her shoulder.

We left Frig at the gate with Lillipuff promising to send a message once we'd returned home. The queen was just finishing her breakfast when we arrived, looking radiant in her cloak of flowers. There was no sign of King Oberon. "Ah. My ladies in waiting—I shall not keep you waiting any longer. We will take the Queen's Road back to Bimblpea and set things to rights."

I looked over at Hollybell and Lillipuff to see if they knew what she was talking about. It seemed they did not. "Your majesty... the Queen's Road?" I asked.

She smiled at the three of us fondly. "Yes. You will see," she said mysteriously. "Now follow me." Titania led us out the gate of the castle and up the slope, towards a scrubby pine tree, the only growing thing visible in the area. As we approached, she began humming, and birdsong surrounded us, filling the air. The tree stretched its stubby, twisted branches out towards us and when we were close enough to touch it, a door opened where none had been before. "Come my ladies, step through while I hold The Queen's Road open."

I took hold of Hollybell's hand, and she took hold of Lillipuff's, and together we stepped through. The Queen followed close behind, and after a short walk through an indescribable landscape, another door appeared. She opened it, and we found ourselves back in the grand hall in Bimblpea where an argument raged amongst the inhabitants.

There was no fanfare or heralds to announce us, and it took a moment before the people in the hall noticed our arrival. Starting in the back nearest us, silence fell, until just the two elders on the dais remained arguing. We could hear them clearly, "She must be dead, or have abandoned us." The argument dropped into the silence like a stone, and finally the two noticed us.

"Fairies of Bimblpea I have not abandoned you. I have come home, through the efforts of your compatriots. They have suffered much, and traveled far to find me." She smiled at the three of us. "Henceforth, they will bow to no one and will be my trusted advisors in all things."

I looked at her in surprise, and she said more quietly, "My dearest friends, I cannot thank you enough for coming to find me. You bow to no one, but tonight I bow to you." She inclined her head toward us, and the fairies in the hall did the same. I stood, mouth agape, uncertain of what to say. Titania chuckled and gave us a wink before turning back to the assembly.

"My people!" She cried, raising her arms to the crowd. "Return to your homes, prepare your dwellings, tell your neighbors, and bring forth your new buds. Tomorrow we will celebrate the Rites of Spring!"

ONE ARROW

Drea Talley

The sun was starting to set. Briony wove through cherry trees heavy with blossoms just off the road, approaching the sprawling manor as lights began to bloom into life through the courtyard. It was a pretty manor, something like an oversized hunting lodge with a more elegant aesthetic. It had two short wings off the main building and numerous large windows and balconies on the second floor. It was so far north that the great forest of Jurai was just beginning to give way to the plains. The manor and the surrounding lands belonged to Lord Albrecht Reige—his summer home, specifically. Lord Reige spent most of the year at his mansion outside the capitol, but came here before the Ides of Spring for the balmy nights and left before the heavy snows.

In the next hour, Lord Reige would finish his dinner and retire to his office, the spacious center room above the great hall with balconies overlooking the forest to the southwest. The lord's ornate desk could be seen easily through the broad windows, which were left open to catch the cool breezes of the evening. Lord Reige went to his office every night after dinner, or so Briony had been assured.

She had paid well for the information. Better than she probably should have. It would be worth it, she promised herself, and reached up to briefly touch the silver and mother-of-pearl locket around her neck. The locket that Moira had given her.

It had been three months since Moira died. The news arrived on a bright and brittle winter morning. Briony had gone numb as her aunt read the letter from Moira's parents. She was killed over some petty rivalry between Lord Reige and a neighboring lord, her last breath spent defending a town that wouldn't notice that the ruler had changed. Briony hadn't gone with her—she didn't want to get involved, and it didn't matter how much money the mercenary company was promising. She'd tried to convince her it was a bad idea. Moira hadn't listened.

Bri, you just don't get it! This is our chance!

It wasn't about the money for her—it was about being a hero, saving the day, making a name for herself. Leaving behind their little farm town on the edge of the woods and finding something better.

Briony had spent the first month blaming herself for not going with Moira, but the pragmatic side of her nature won out. Briony was excellent with a bow, and knew the woods better than anyone short of the elves that lived in the heart of the forest, but that wouldn't have helped much in a border skirmish. No, the blame wasn't hers. It fell upon the ridiculous lords who thought the lives of soldiers were worth less than their egos. It fell upon the man who sent his soldiers to that small village to kill the team of fresh faced recruits just to expand his land by a handful of acres.

The last of the lights on either side of the great main gate flared to life as Briony approached her destination. Across from the main gate, on the other side of the road, was a great oak tree that rose above the softly pink clouds of cherry blossoms and stretched towards the sky. The timing was important. The lowest branches, the ones Briony could reach, were on the side of the tree facing the gate. The guard was about to change, however. She watched, still and quiet, as the number of guards briefly swelled from two to six, but they chatted amongst themselves for a moment. That was her opportunity. She jumped up, catching the lowest branch, and clenched her teeth as she pulled herself up onto it. As soon as she got up, she began to climb around to the backside of the tree, away from the road.

It had taken over a month and a half to track down Lord Reige. In truth, finding him had not been difficult, the lord was hardly secretive about his whereabouts. It was getting there. Briony made the journey mostly on foot, camping in the woods or sleeping in barns. Carriages were expensive, and she didn't know how much money she would need once she arrived. Winter had also hampered her travel, causing her to lose days on the road as she waited out a storm.

By all the Gods, Bri, just buy a horse! It had been a frequent comment from Moira—Briony was good with animals, and her aunt had the land and a stable. One more horse wouldn't have been an imposition.

Briony hadn't wanted the responsibility. Besides, Moira's horse was a powerhouse, so she just rode behind Moira. Briony was svelte and petite. Almost a head shorter than her friend, she didn't slow them down.

Two more weeks to get to know some of the servants, learn their patterns, and find the ones who waited on the lord. A lot of nights paying for others' drinks in the local tavern so they would relax enough to be honest with her.

If you wanna make friends, Bri, buy a round.

The worst had been the huntmaster's assistant. Wandering hands and horrible teeth, the drinks had not been enough. Briony had to smile and pretend she would let him follow her back to her inn. She got the information, though. Before she'd left the handsy bastard unconscious in a ditch to wake up with a headache he could blame on the alcohol.

All of it led to this enormous oak on the edge of the northern forests of Jurai, two days before the Ides of Spring. A great tree with a trunk wider than a man could wrap his arms around, and sturdy branches that could easily support a woman just under nine stones. Briony found the branch she had been looking for, almost as wide as she was and pointing straight at the second floor of the manor. Hauling herself up, she sat down on the broad limb and leaned back against the trunk to catch her breath. Soon it would be over, and she would be in the woods away from this place before Lord Reige's guards realized anything was amiss. For now, there was nothing to do but wait.

Briony impatiently strummed her bowstring, staring at the window. How long had it taken her to get up the tree? She wasn't sure. She couldn't track the moon from here, her view obstructed by the new leaves. Those same leaves hid her well. Still, it was impossible not to feel anxious as time slowly passed.

There was movement in the room, and Briony's head picked up. "Finally," she muttered, and pushed forward away from the trunk, getting to her feet and creeping carefully further out onto the branch. She knew how far she could go, how long the branch would support her. It was further than one might think.

Servants swept through the room, turning up lamps and setting down a tray of what looked like tea on the edge of the desk, then they left just as quickly. Albion Reige arrived just behind them. He was young for a lord, not having quite reached his 30th year. Briony settled into place, down on one knee, the other bent before her to keep her stable and steady. She pulled three arrows from the quiver at her hip. The first one should kill him, but if for any reason she didn't quite hit her mark she would follow with the other two. Lord Reige's desk faced the interior of the room. His back was to the wide, open window.

"Arrogant fool," Briony said with bite, and took a deep breath as she nocked the arrow and drew back the bow. She let the breath out slowly as she took aim.

Bri, what in the Nine Hells are you doing!?

Briony froze, bow still drawn. "I …"

I thought you didn't want to be a killer!

That was what she had told Moira before her friend took the company's money and left for the nameless town she died in. That she didn't want to be a killer. That hunting was one thing, but these were people, with families. And best friends. Moira had said she didn't understand, that it was about helping the villagers. Briony had responded that helping the villagers still meant killing soldiers.

Briony's eyes began to fill with tears.

Only fools confuse vengeance and justice.

Tears flowed down Briony's cheeks as she stayed there, bow drawn, until her arms started to ache. Until her aim started to drift from the fatigue and her tear-blurred vision. Until Lord Reige stood, turned down the lamps at his desk, and moved away from the window, ruining her shot. It was then that Briony's arms came down, and she tucked the arrows back into her quiver with trembling hands. More tears fell as she slung the bow over her shoulder before inching back along the branch. She kept crying as she sat on the wide branch again, leaning back against the tree.

Killing Albion Reige wouldn't bring Moira back. It wouldn't even make Briony feel better. And the lord would die quickly, having no idea who killed him or why it mattered. The most beautiful girl with the brightest laugh would still be gone, and a new lord would step up to replace the old one.

The tears came faster now, and Briony was racked by sobs. She hadn't cried since Moira died. It seemed that was what she had come here to do.

THE RHYTHM OF THUNDER

Juliet Wilde

One: Falling Rains

The peoples come for First Rains when the skies burst with fresh waters. They travel from the towns to revel in the abundant flows after the long, dry winter. On big beasties, on wagons, and on feet, they arrive to witness the resurgence of the rivers that replenish the lands in the valley until the next dry season. They gather to celebrate me.

At night, when starlight dances on the surface of the wellspring, they make camps along the cool waters nestled against the rocky cliffs. I watch from the trees, the ledges, and the center of the well as they dance by the fires and feast on the fresh meat they have hunted. All the peoples bask in the rich, earthy scent of petrichor after the first rain. I pad barefoot among them, unseen, over the soft earth and rock in the shade of lush trees.

In the morning, they strip down to unders, dark-colored braies and shifts that cling to bodies when they swim. The youngers play naked, splashing in the creek, while the olders bathe in the deep waters of the well. Olders and youngers alike dare each other to cross the watery chasm, darting glances toward the bottomless pool. The cautious stay clear from the edge and bathe in the flowing waters fed from the springs. Families with paddling totlings and kicking babelets wade downriver in the burbling eddies.

Older children climb the face of the rock to peer into the well. Some stand mesmerized, working up the courage to jump. The bravest do not pause to consider the depth before throwing themselves in.

Most cannot resist the pull of the spring with the inviting crisp, green waters. They do not know how deep it is. Toys and tools have never reached the bottom. The rocky walls within the well are crystal clear. The surface is so smooth the cliffs beneath look like a reflection of the rock walls towering above. So clear, the peoples can see all the way down to where the shaft angles into lightlessness to flow beneath the cliffs. So close, the peoples can almost touch it, but the few who try never resurface.

One people, the bravest of them, with graceful arms and legs and wide brown eyes, scales the wall and stands at the precipice. Not a moment of doubt crosses the sun-kissed face before he launches himself from the rocks. He dives headfirst, a pointed arrow that slices the surface with a slight ripple.

The resonating around me stills as he pierces the green-blue water to plummet to a depth almost as deep as anyone has reached before and lived. I watch to make sure I do not have to spit the daring one out.

He scrambles out of the water and scales the limestone ledges to return to the precipice.

"Set an example, Croft," a mama calls from the edge of the pool. "You know the children look up to you."

Croft. The name of the daring one.

He waves, and before he can suppress a lip-quirk, he launches himself into another graceful dive. Someone wading in the creek below laughs.

Bubbles effervesce around him, minnows scatter, and water envelops him as energy ripples down the length of the watery tunnel. When he emerges, a younger asks, "How did you do that?"

A younger child waiting on the cliff—not too much younger, but young enough to swim without a shift—asks, "Can I jump with you, brudder?"

"Jump after me," he says, stooping to level gazes with the small one. "I'll wait for you."

She beams a bright and admiring smile.

He dives. At the surface, he treads the waters to wait. "Feet first," he calls to her.

The young one drops with flailing limbs and an impressive splash. Croft swims with her when she emerges, and they climb out together to scale the wall again.

At the top of the rocks, he grins, revealing a hint of self-satisfied mischief that tickles me. As the wave of joy flushes through me, the boskage resonates with a surge of energy. The foliage flushes, the leaves brighten, and the sweet scent of fresh green flourishes.

The intense gaze of Croft snaps to study the trees where I stand.

Does he notice them?

He scans the trees near me, gaze stopping to peer into the foliage as if he is looking straight at me. I feel the intense stare like the heat of a ray of light through the trees.

Does he see me?

How curious.

He backs up and disappears behind a cluster of boulders only to reappear on the path leading away from where the peoples camp.

"Where you going?" a chorus of voices calls after him.

"Be right back," he says, never glancing away from the trees or the speckled light playing amongst them.

Steady of foot, he climbs onto a ledge that hugs the rock face. He sidesteps along the ledge, body pressed against the wall, calculating the placement of each step. He is careful on the rock, but fearless. Like a young buck who has learned to wield the antlers of a new season.

He stops to peer through the lush greenery of the canopy behind him while he navigates the ledge. As he approaches, I dissolve into mist and reform, unseen, near him. Furrowing a brow, he glances back to study the wall.

I follow him, enjoying watching the bravado as he finds the crevice in the face of the rock and wanders in. Only the most curious do. He leans into the narrow gap, peering into the darkness. A moment later, he edges into the dark space.

The light illuminates the entrance of the cave, but he moves into the shadows and stops. After a moment, he walks deeper, taking time to adjust to the dark. As he turns to look back, a sliver of light flashes over him to reveal a wide, mischievous grin and dimpled cheek. Then he disappears into the black.

I follow, drifting along the wall, close enough to watch but invisible. He sniffs the air, scenting the pleasant damp, metallic rock surrounding him, cool and clean. In this small, close space, he has an energy that vibrates the air and wraps around me.

He closes big brown eyes and cocks an inquisitive head to the side before he pivots like a flower turning toward the sun. When he faces me, he grins.

Is he sensing me? The feeling is strange. To be seen, though he cannot.

The life in the forest—the boskage and the beasties—sense me, but that is more from a sharing of energy. They feel the energy that is me the way they anticipate rain when the air pressure changes or intuit whether to run or hide when a toothy beastie is stalking them.

Brown eyes open and blink a few times, but narrow shoulders hunch when he sees nothing. He scans the short distance before him. He cannot see me, but he knows I am here.

Such a rare one.

I have never felt loneliness until now. For the first time in a long time, I remember what it is to be seen, or sensed, by another.

Maybe it is because I feel seen. Maybe it is because he is brave.

Like me, this adventurous one is content with solitude.

Maybe that is why he can sense me.

Gathering the energy that is me from the vapor in the air, I take solid form and appear in people-shape before him. Those big eyes widen to the size of great-horned-owl eyes and focus on the physical presence in front of him.

I sometimes see myself reflected in the crystalline pools of the dark caverns below. I know how I appear, but I never see myself reflected in the eyes of others. Shades of jade green, agate blue, amber brown, and smoke gray ebb and flow in swirls over skin that echoes the features of the natural world I inhabit. The colors ripple and eddy as if reflecting light on water. The phosphorescence of the colorful skin illuminates the cave walls, and casts us in undulating waves of blue green light.

Croft rewards me with wide-eyed, slack-jawed admiration.

I am as naked as the forest in winter, but light and color dance and flow over me, casting shadows and textures that, like the surface of the well outside, prevent seeing into the depths. The effect offers enough covering that the boy does not balk or tremble at the form he sees.

"Your skin looks like water," he says, reaching out to touch the belly of me. He stops before connecting with the skin, and I laugh when he gazes up. "You're beautiful." The whisper is loud in the enclosed space.

"Thank you," I say, charmed by the candor of the bold one.

"Who... what are you?"

"I am Sehli Wehkya."

"Silly?" he asks.

I chuckle and repeat the name. "Sehli."

"What does it mean?"

The answer comes slow because it is not something that *means*. It is something that is. It is me. Finally, as he looks on, I say, "Whispering Waters."

"Are you a witch, Silly?" With a hand held aloft, he seems to debate whether to touch the shifting colors on the surface of the belly.

"Of sorts, I suppose."

"Do you eat people?"

That makes me chuckle again. To talk to someone—to share a name—fills me with lightness. The peoples from the towns are always fearful of things they cannot understand.

"No," I say. "I care for the forest here. Are you scared of me?"

Expressive eyes draw together as he considers before answering. "No. Do you live here alone? In this cave?"

"I am not alone," I say, charmed by this inquisitive explorer. "I have the boskage and beasties and rocks for company."

"The rocks? They keep you company?"

"As much as I keep the company of the selfsame me."

Mouth dropping open as he lets out a pensive little sigh, he considers this. *Can he feel the hum of the rocks and the flow of water the way he can sense me?* I believe he can.

"The forest is my home," I say, "but I dwell with the water."

Seeming to notice the tan hand he holds between us, he lowers it. We stand in amicable silence, sharing company.

The undulating and whirling colors of the skin brighten before him, casting more vibrant light within the crevice to reveal the length of the corridor and an opening at the end. It is rare for anything other than bats or salamanders to venture so deep into this rock. I glow brighter still at sharing this quiet place with one so appreciative.

"Would you like to see?" I ask.

Eyes sparkle at me in the dim light.

"Come," I say, extending a hand to him.

He takes it with the same fearlessness that propelled him headfirst off the cliffs outside.

At the edge of the tunnel, we look across the cavern that spreads out before us. In the center is a pool. The air is still here, and no sound can be heard from the waters or peoples outside. Only the little gasp that escapes him disturbs the silence. He turns to look at me, and I smile, curious what he must think of this hidden well. It is a long time since I have enjoyed sharing the wonder of it. This company, curious and open, fills the well of solitude I live with.

I did not know solitude could be companionable. I find I like the sharing.

Only the still surface is illuminated by the light I emit. Beneath, it is black. He steps into the pool, disturbing the stillness and sending ripples that reflect the light I shine. I catch the little quirk of lips, and then he is gone. He dives into that black water.

Fearless.

I dive in after him, once again awed by the pluck of this people. So unlike the peoples who pray to me for water, who cower in the dark, who dare not tread amongst the unknown.

When we surface, he says, "My name is Croft." Then as quick as he makes the announcement, he swims toward the center of the pool, surrounded on all sides by rock wall.

I do not tell him I know this from listening to the peoples outside, but I follow him. He splashes about as I brighten to illuminate the walls and the water beneath.

The light only penetrates so deep. Face pressed into the surface, he peers into the abyss. When he looks up, he asks, "How deep is this pool?"

"Not as deep as the pool outside, but deep," I say, suspended in the water. No need to tread. I am the water.

"How deep is the pool outside? No one has ever touched the bottom."

"Would you like to see?"

"It's not possible."

"With me it is. But you must not tell a soul."

"No one would believe me."

I leave it at that. No one *would* believe him. But worse, if they did, they might try, and there are enough bones littering the depths of the well.

Illuminating the water, I descend, lighting the way as I swim. The still black becomes ripples of greens, blues, and silvers. Behind me, the energy from Croft radiates through the water as he flips and follows me. Fearless.

I reach a narrow gap along the side wall some way down. When I breach the gap, apprehension trembles off him again, but he shakes it off, ease exuding from him once more.

He is comfortable with the unknown. Or maybe it is that he feels safe with me, accepting that air for the lungs is not a concern. With me, he is simply matter existing among the elements.

I lead him into the fissure, a passage so tight we cannot advance with wide strokes but must grip the smoothed limestone walls to pull forward. Soon, I emerge from the fissure into an open space. When the light spreads out to illuminate another vast cavern, I feel him behind me, hands resting on the shoulders I offer for support. I marvel at the contact. To be touched is like to be seen, and once again I recognize loneliness only from its absence.

He peers over me to see a whole world below the one he knows. Wonder ripples through the water. Eager, he swims around me to explore.

Palms up, he flashes me a look. *Is this real?* The questioning expression is as nuanced as the shades of coloring on the rock walls.

Brightening to illuminate the cavern and show off the swirling formations, I urge him to explore, and he kicks away. He disappears behind an enormous stalactite formed by centuries of water eddying through this chamber. He swims back to me, and when I make to follow, he leads the way in exploration, confident despite being submerged within a pocket of water far from any access to the surface.

A short time later, I direct him to follow me again. I descend lower, finding another smooth fissure in the rock. This time we swim along a flat passageway, solid rock above and below us. I shine, creating a bubble of light as black water shrinks the space ahead and behind. The apprehension radiating off him is perceptible but slight.

At the end of the narrow pass, we emerge into another shaft, this one at an angle. I illuminate the juncture, revealing rocks, ironware, toys, and bones and skulls of beasties and peoples littering the ground. Flicking a glance at me and then down again, comprehension flares in the wide brown eyes fixed on the floor.

Drawn by a dim light ahead, he moves to dart upward, but I grip him by an arm and gesture with finger to lips. *I am a secret.* He nods and swims alongside me. I quiet the phosphorescence as the tunnel bends upward and natural sunlight pours in through the hole above.

Wonder ripples the water between us when a splash booms then effervesces at the surface, sending waves that envelop us all the way down here. Then another. And another. The silhouettes of kicky peoples cross the aperture of blue light overhead. I feel rather than hear the little gasp from Croft next to me. When I look at him, he is beaming, the little dimple in the cheek twinkly in the blue rays.

He grows restless, and I gesture for us to return. As we swim back to the fissure below, a red-spotted sunfish the size of a people-palm swims past the exuberant face of the curious one. When he laughs, he releases a bubble of air that makes him laugh harder. Joy reverberates in the water surrounding us.

Together, we navigate the return journey through the dim passage, vast cavern, and secret well until we surface inside the dark rock.

"You live in here?" he asks, unleashing a deluge of questions all the way through the dark passage to the outside ledge. "How can I breathe under there?" he says without taking a breath, and I wonder how he can breathe out *here*.

"Do you take sacrifices?" he asks, and I remember the look he flashed when he saw the bones and skulls along the floor of the well.

"I do not require them. But sometimes they are offered by those who forget the power I wield. It serves as a reminder to others."

Unfazed, he lets another question loose. "Can I come back to visit?"

"Of course," I say, navigating the narrow corridor. I dim the luminescence as we reach the sunlit opening, allowing the eyes of the boy to adjust to the bright sky.

When we emerge, we are greeted by the screech of a hawk overhead, cicadas chirring in the trees, and the vibrant sounds of life on the ground. Croft quiets, as if recognizing the end of the adventure.

"I am always here," I say. "You can visit me whenever you like."

"This is our secret," he says, confirming that he has witnessed something that is for him alone. I believe he understands, though I do not know why. Whether it is the fearlessness, the company, or the vibrant energy he shares with me. Maybe it is that he sees me.

He hugs the rocks as he sidesteps the way back along the ledge.

"Where have you been?" a sunny voice booms as he emerges from the path. The youngers circle him when he meets them at the precipice. "We were coming to look for you."

"Just looking around," he says, joining the peoples. A pensive quiet replaces the chattering exuberance he showed me as he listens to the others boast about the many jumps and all he has missed.

From a perch nearby, I watch him and the friend-peoples revel in the abundant waters. Olders call after youngers, the youngest leap from river rock to river rock, and couples lounge on the edge of the water. They throw themselves from the rocks as the boskage of spring flourishes everywhere. The well is deep, and the waters flow freely.

Croft looks back to the place where I sit.

TWO: ABUNDANT SPRINGS

They come to celebrate the abundant waters that ensure the towns thrive after the long, dry winter. They come to connect with the wild and remember primal beginnings. They come to join with the hum of everything. I pad, unseen, among the pilgrims who linger after the first scurries of peoples have come and gone.

The sleek form of a people slicing the air catches the attention of all, especially me. The dive is captivating, headlong and sleek.

I watch from a nearby branch as the muscular body pierces the water, leaving a modest ripple on the surface. When he reemerges, he swims with elegant strokes to the edge of the pool. There is something familiar about this self-possessed people that draws the admiration of those who look on. The smile is broad, and he has a dimple.

The face is no longer soft round, but the sculpted face of a man. Croft. The hair is darker, but the waves are the same, slicked back from the face.

He pulls himself from the well, and I cannot help noticing the changes to the body as water sluices off him. Taller and stronger. He climbs the cliffs again but stops to scan the foliage around the creek. Head cocked to the side, he squints to scan the area where I am perched. For a moment, the perceptive gaze lands on me, but he seems to see through me.

Intuition tells him I am here. He senses me, which makes me smile. A vibrant joy flushes through me, and as I preen at being seen, the foliage near me flourishes.

"Croft," a voice calls from the cliffs, breaking the intense scrutiny.

"Coming," he calls back. Muscular back, taut buttocks, and strong legs flex and strain as he climbs the rock wall.

I dissipate into mist and reform on the cliff to watch from the tree line. I remember the daring one who once saw me. I drift, relocating myself on the precipice next to him.

A fresh energy quivers and tightens in the center of me. No apprehension vibrates off him, though, as he reaches upward. With a slight bend of the knees, he launches himself headfirst into the air.

I relocate to the center well and wait for him. At the depth of the plunge, he flips to return to the surface, but I grip him by the arm before he can ascend. The colors of the water—jade, agate, amber, and silver—ripple over me, hair the color of limestone waving around me as I take people-shape before him. Suspended in water, we face one another.

The big brown eyes do not widen in surprise, but he gives a mischievous grin. I raise a finger to gaping lips. A *secret*, I remind him. He nods quickly before I dissolve into the light of the water.

The peoples above call to him when he resurfaces. "How deep did you go this time?" one asks.

"Too deep," Croft answers.

I relocate to stand, unseen, next to him when he lifts out of the pool. "I don't recommend it," he says. "I almost didn't come back up."

"We're not that brave, anyway," another voice calls

"Or stupid," a third voice adds, and they all laugh.

When he begins to climb, I relocate to the cliff to wait for him. The energy is electric like thunder on the wind. Anticipation. He pauses at the top of the cliff and looks around him as if trying to find a hidden object.

After chatting with the friend-peoples for a moment and watching some jump—none brave enough to dive headfirst—he backs away, scanning the trees around the precipice.

I watch as he slips, unnoticed, to follow the narrow ledge that hugs the rock between the face and the canopy.

Arriving at the crevice in the face of the rock, he steps into the shadows. "When I was a boy, I thought I dreamed you," he says, knowing I am here. He touches the walls as he moves deeper into the rock.

"You did not dream me," I say. I take shape in the exact place he is looking—the place where he senses I am. Curious, this people who can feel the energy of me. "I am real."

The brown-eyed gaze holds steady on the colorful face before him before finally glancing down to the swirls of colors flowing over the people-shape I reveal to him. The eyes linger there a long while. This time, I do not laugh at the curious wonder of youth. Rather, this appreciative admiration of a mature people stirs other feelings in me. I face the perceptiveness of a grown-people.

The gaze snaps back up, and the air grows hot, coloring olive-skinned cheeks. I extend a hand to him, and he takes it, accepting the invitation to another adventure.

I lead him along the corridor until we emerge at the inner well to stand on the ledge overlooking the black pool. He does not dive in the way he did before. Instead, he grips the hand he holds and faces the water before us. Together, we jump.

When we splash in the water, I brighten to illuminate the effervescent bubbles tickling us as they rise. Suspended beneath the surface, we face each other. I gesture below, inviting him to take the lead. He knows the way. He dives to the gap in the wall.

Casting enough light for him to see ahead, I follow him into the narrow gash, and we pull ourselves through the tight passage until we emerge in the great cavern at the other end. Cycles before, I watched him play. Now, he studies the undulating patterns of layered rock.

I gesture upward and grasp a hand. He follows with little prompting, and we surface within the caverns. The water is lower this year, so this chamber is not a solid cell of water. When we reach the edge of the pool, there is a slope where we can crawl out. On the rock shelf, I illuminate to cast light over the entire cavern. The pillar Croft once swam around, one of many formations shaped by the waters, reaches the ceiling. There are other fissures in the rock above where water drips to ripple in the pool.

The younger Croft spent all the time he spent here in the water. Now this Croft studies the ceiling, the fissures that pass overhead. The smooth curving of the rock walls that mark the passing of time and water.

Could he conceive of the times that I have witnessed? That I have shaped?

He scans the space briefly, curious, but an appreciative gaze returns to settle on the solid shape I have formed.

"You are as beautiful as I remember."

An unfamiliar flush of warmth flows through me. "You are more so," I say, not bashful about looking at the broad shoulders.

He smiles sweetly, revealing a shyness that I would not expect from the swaggering young man who dives headlong into chilly abysses and disappears with mysterious entities. A bloom of heat trembles in the air and ripples over us.

I am curious about the life he has lived. The cycles that have passed. How has he changed? What does the life of a people in the towns look like?

"What is it like for you in the town?" I ask.

"My pa is still farming, but he sent me to the city to study to learn building. Such skills are needed in the towns," he says, taking a seat at the edge of the water. "You've been here all along."

I join him, dangling feet in the water next to him. "Here and in the forest."

"I dreamt about this place, about you, since that visit. I'd've come back sooner if I thought you were real. I mean, I'd hoped ..."

He glances across the water. "How is it I can be here? Breathe in the water for so long?"

I had answered the question before, but like the grown people standing before me, the curiosity of the man is also bigger and more nuanced.

"The same way you can see me, I suppose." I reach out, pressing a hand against the sun-kissed skin over where the heart beats. "You can sense the energy of life forces around you. The beasties and the boskage sense me in the wild. Not many are able to see me unless I want them to."

"Before she died, my ma used to say that I'd be a wolf if they hadn't forced me to sleep inside." Arms draped casually over knees, he faces me with a coy smile. "I never told a soul."

"Would they have believed you?" I ask. "You could have been talking of dreams."

The playfulness of youth peeks through in the wide smile set in the face of this man with an angular jaw and high cheekbones. "It was my dream to keep. One I treasured. It was my special secret."

I lean against the side of him, and he remains still, face close to me, a spider lying in wait. He lures me, and I press forward to satisfy the niggling curiosity. I press hungry lips to full, pouty ones, and he responds, inviting me to explore him. He draws me in to learn more through kisses.

Enjoying this game, I pull back to whisper, "You are a grown-people."

"I'm glad you noticed," he says, closing the narrow gap between us.

The kisses linger a long while, the warmth of soft flesh pressing together, feeling. Playing. The earthy hum of pleasure ignites the air around us, soft but fierce, full-bodied but bubbly. Enthralling. The silence in the cavern is interrupted only by dripping water and the wet sounds of lips and tongues meeting.

It is a long time before we part and return to the water to play.

Descending, we find the gap in the rock that leads to the well outside. When we reach it, we emerge into the beams of midday light penetrating the crystal waters. We swim with minnows and red-spotted sunfish. A salamander scuttles along the wall beneath us. Croft picks up a tiny metal horse he spies among the river rock, lost items, and bones littering the tunnel.

In the crystalline depths, he pulls me against him to steal another kiss, which I surrender to with full-bodied eagerness. We wrestle and play. Holding hands, we descend deeper along the tunnel to where light does not reach. He grabs onto an ankle as I swim away, but when I dissolve into invisible energy, he cannot grab onto me. He senses me in the water around him and gives chase, and we return to the light. He enjoys the game, though I am not easy to catch.

I like being caught, as much as I like being seen.

It is a long while before we retrace our steps to return to the friend-peoples gathered above.

As the sun sweeps overhead, the light changes in the same way that I shift energy. Peoples sit on the precipice, dangling feet over the edge to watch the sunset. Unseen, I sit with him, listening to the talk, silently laughing at the jokes, though some I do not understand. I preen when they appreciate the forest around them, and dewdrops well on the foliage nearby.

Croft feels me behind him the way I sense him, but I am a secret. He no longer needs to scan the surroundings to find me. The energy that connects him with the earth ties him to me.

I join the peoples for the night celebrations and enjoy the revelries from my place in the shadow cast by Croft in the firelight. I flow in the water around him when they swim, I melt into the rock beneath him, and I cling to the water drops that trickle over him.

When the friend-peoples retire for the night, pair off into private celebrations, or simply fall asleep where they sit, Croft leaves the camp and climbs up to the cliff. I meet him at the top overlooking the waters that reflect the stars and the flicker of dying fires.

"I would have come sooner," he says.

"I enjoy watching you with the friend-peoples," I say, meaning it.

"Do you travel to the towns?"

"No." It would be easy to flow with the water to find them, but the energy there is chaos. There is no place for me. The peoples keep the lands and animals, and there are those like me that inhabit the shadows and waters and greens and energies. There is no need for me in the towns. I would feel crowded there.

We linger and talk, kiss and touch, and eventually sleep

under the stars. In the morning, he returns to the friend-peoples. I accompany him, unseen, as they pack the camp and ready the big pack beasties to journey home.

"I'll come see you," he says softly in a quiet moment away from the friend-peoples. I press invisible fingers to soft lips, and the wide smile of the man energizes the air where we touch. There is no mischief in the eyes that look back as he rides away. Just a melancholy when he glances at the place where I stand, unseen.

The lifespan of a people is not the same as that of a goddess of the wild. I take the promise for what it is, a wishful thought. I treasure it and let him go.

THREE: VIOLENT FLOWS

First Rains are late this year. Though water levels are low, the boskage draws deep, and the beasties are resourceful. And, of course, they have me. There is always water in the well, even if the creeks run dry.

Deep in the caverns, I bathe in the echo of chirps and clicks emanating from the ceiling where hairless bat pups cluster for warmth and wait for the mamas to find and nurse them. Older pups drop into the dark by the thousands and zip around to navigate the space amongst the others. I watch hopeful for each squeaking pup, though many collide in the chaos and fall into the collective maw of the carnivorous beetles waiting on the cave floor.

When a percussive force reverberates through the rock walls, the cheeps and flutters halt, and for a moment, all is silent. I emerge from the cave to an unfamiliar clanging that echoes off the trees and rocks and assaults the senses. Boskage roots tense in the earth, and little beasties freeze in place.

As I pad through the forest, the vibrations in the earth flow into me and resonate in my being with each blow. When I advance on the source of the clanging, I dissipate into the air and relocate to the source of the unrest.

A scurry of peoples gathers where an old, long-dry streambed veers from the main creek. But these are not the pilgrims coming for First Rains. They are not here for celebration. The peoples hurry around like worker ants.

When I find the source of the clanging, it is iron on stone as peoples swing tools and tear into the ground. Nearby, pack beasties and wagons are unloaded, the tools, canvas bundles, and wooden barrels set on the ground. Peoples slash at the dry brush growing along the creek, not yet touched by the rains. Tents and cook fires are tended downstream. Little flags made of natural cloth tied to stakes pierce the ground along a trench dug into the dry bed. More little flags are spiked into the ground around a hole. I pad, unseen, toward peoples standing in a circle looking down into the hole.

Like a cool breeze, I approach from behind to investigate the people who commands the attention of the worker-peoples. The commanding one gestures to a section of the trench, showing the peoples holding iron axpikes and longspades where to break through rock and where to dig. The bracing yet relaxed stance of him is familiar, and I am unable to look away.

He is tall, hair tied back in a ponytail. The face is shadowed by a hat made of deer hide, but the tunic he wears is simple and dirt-smeared like those of the worker-peoples. He stands a head taller than the tallest, but it is the assertive voice that holds the influence. The peoples listen, gazes trained on the land where he gestures. When he continues to another scurry of worker-peoples, this group resumes the clanging.

Formless, I gravitate toward him among the peoples. I halt when I hear voices from below and peer into the hole to find more peoples with axpikes and longspades at the bottom. Digging.

Another well?

When the commanding one turns into the sun, there is no dimple or mischievous grin, but the profile is unmistakable. Lines around the eyes tally the years, but it is him. Croft. At the collar hangs a little metal horse on a leather cord. The young man, now older, is more solid, thicker, and still beautiful.

How many cycles have passed?

I watch, unseen, at the edge of the dredged earth, unable to look away from him. He speaks to the peoples as they dig, breaking through the limestone, dredging the earth, clanging against the rock. The strong back stiffens, and the sculpted chin tilts upward and stills, like a beastie scenting the air. As the peoples around him ask questions, he pivots to face the air I occupy. He does not see me, but I sense the knowing radiating off him. He feels the presence of me.

With an amicable slap on the back of one worker, he mutters instructions to the scurry. "I'll be back," he says, and then he walks toward the brush.

"You want us to come with you, Chief?" a people calls after him.

"No, no. I know these woods. I'll be fine," he says and disappears into the shadows of the boskage.

If it were not for the sound of breaking twigs and crunching leaves beneath the heavy boots, he might have vanished into the air. Like me. He cuts a straight line to the creek, and I trail behind him until he emerges from the foliage onto the creek bank upstream from where the worker-peoples clang.

He does not glance behind as he stalks upriver, but I catch glimpses of an upturned cheek or a tilt of the head as we walk toward the well. When we are far enough away that only the echoes of the clanging ring in the trees, he turns to face me. The mouth opens as if to speak, but he stays silent, gazing hard at the air where I stand.

Unseen, this body remembers the pleasure of being sensed by another, and I resonate as I appear before him in the people-shape that is me.

"You're here," he says in a breathless whisper.

"I am always here," I say simply. I cannot fathom where else I would be.

To match the cycles Croft has lived, the form I take is thicker, like the mama-peoples that come for First Rains. Instead of lines around the eyes, the colors that roll over me now are those of rippling water under a setting sun—golden, orange, and pink.

"You're as beautiful as I remember you," he says, not moving. "But you're real."

"You are also beautiful," I say, warmed by the unfamiliar flush of being seen by appreciative eyes. Excitement charges the air between us.

We walk the rest of the way toward the wellspring where the peoples will soon come to celebrate First Rains.

"What are you digging for?" I ask as we amble along the creek.

"We're building an aqueduct," he says, holding an arm out for me.

"A quaduct?" I ask as I hook an arm around the one he offers. He is thicker than he was as a young man. He has a bit of a belly, and he is strong.

When he chuckles, it is a low rumble. "Yes. A quaduct. It's like a creek. To bring water to the towns." There is warmth in the hand that rests on me, and the energy vibrating between us is a welcome one.

"Peoples make creeks? Is there not enough water?"

"The towns are growing," he says, turning serious. "And so is the need for water. Waiting until Spring Rains is like waiting for a mystery to reveal itself. The unknown of waiting means life or death when farmers start planting crops for the growing season."

"This is what you do now? Build creeks?"

How odd that there would not be enough water, that the peoples would need to build creeks.

"Mostly. I have other jobs, but I'm charged with the business of water."

"Water is not business," I say, indignant. *Water is life. How could it be business?*

"It is," he says, but there is a note of sadness. "I prefer to be designing and building around water. That's the fun part of my work. I build bridges, dams, and reservoirs, but the business of water is a necessity for the survival of the city. It occupies all my time."

"And what of your family? Do you spend time with them?"

"My family is large. My brothers and sisters—do you remember them?"

"I do. All the little chicklings followed you everywhere, even over the cliff."

He laughs, the lines around the eyes scrunching up. "Yes, they did. They are all grown now with their own chicklings," he says on another rolling chuckle. "I was married, but my wife passed several years ago, leaving me with my own chicklings. They are mostly grown, too, which leaves me time for building."

Curious about the customs of the peoples, I ask, "You did not find another wife?"

"No," he says, squeezing the arm pressed against him, the little mischievous glint returning. "Raising my chicklings and the business of water kept me too busy."

When we arrive at the well, the strong shoulders relax, and he guides me directly to the rock wall overlooking the well. He climbs it without so much as a glance around, and I dissolve into vapor and float to the top to wait for him.

"You are responsible for the peoples in the towns?" I ask when he reaches the top. The work does not surprise me. Even as a boy, the peoples listened to him and followed him.

He does not answer but looks over the cliff and into the well below. At length, he says, "Not all the people, but I am charged with making sure we have water for our crops. And that we can distribute food for all the town and city folk."

"Me too," I say simply.

He gives me a funny look. Now it is my turn to chuckle. I imagine he thinks I spend the cycles wandering the forest, contemplating the ripples in the light and the seeds on the wind.

"Does it bother you, us taking your water?" he asks as he strips down to braies, leaving the cord with the tiny horse in place around the neck.

"Bother? Why should I be bothered? Water is for all. It is not *my* water. I do not create it. It is energy. It is not mine to keep or give."

"Energy?" He bundles the clothes into a tidy roll, and I follow to where he tucks the roll into a depression in a nearby boulder.

"Life is energy. Everything has energy," I say. "Rocks have life, energy." I press my hand against the boulder. "They have a birth and a death and a rebirth cycle."

"Like the peoples?" he asks, again with a mischievous smile. Pulling me by the hand, he returns to the cliff.

"Like the peoples," I confirm. "You laugh because the peoples—and the beasties and boskage—do not witness the lives of the rocks." Though I do not think that is truly the reason he is laughing, he does not correct me.

Holding hands, we sit on the edge of the cliff. He sits facing me, one leg dangling over the edge. He waits, the mischievous little grin gone, transformed into a pensive line, listening with the same intense focus he had even as a boy.

"The birth of stone like this..." I place my hand flat on the limestone rock beneath us. "...begins as grit and earth and water, compressed by time and the weight of the cycles that came before, until it becomes solid. Then the forces of more time break down the hard stone, and it becomes grit again. Life is energy."

He gazes at the interlaced fingers between us as I talk.

"A golden-eyed burbler bird eats a berry, then the little beastie dumps the seed when he flies. The seed becomes a tree. A red-winged dinal builds a nest in the tree, and the red-winged babelets grow up to eat more berries."

I trace the veins along the fingers of the strong hands that hold mine, admiring the swirling jades, blues, and ambers of skin that resembles water against the tan skin of rough hands that resemble limestone.

"The tree dies," I say. "Mushrooms make a home. In time, the tree becomes the grit of the earth. A red-winged dinal in flight dumps a seed. Because of all the birds and seeds and worms and mushrooms that came before it, a seedling in the dirt sprouts a new tree, strong and tall."

A surprised gaze snaps to me. "The forest is a busy place."

"Water makes it busier," I say. "It is energy. Water will always flow, the life energy will always move through the rocks, the beasties, the boskage. That is my charge. That is the way of it everywhere. The way you want to move water—energy—for the peoples."

I cannot read the expression the face makes. The smirk is gone. Instead, the mouth hangs open.

I mimic the gape-lipped expression the way still water reflects the sky. He surprises me with a booming laugh that echoes.

"Energy," he whispers with a little head shake. Then he leans forward to press a quick kiss to the lips that tease him. "Show me." He stands up and tugs me by the hand.

We are still holding hands when we jump into the well.

In the water, we descend until we find the bend in the tunnel where it becomes dark. I illuminate the path as we reach the crevice in the rock wall and enter. Gliding through the dim, craggy corridor, I look back to see him studying the walls with a look of wonder.

Then he turns that wondrous gaze to me, and I cannot help but flush at the warmth. Such a silly thing to glow at simply being seen.

At the surface of the inner pool, we climb out to recline at the edge of the water. He pulls me to lie back against him, and we listen to absolute silence.

"We'll be working nearby for a few weeks," he says, interrupting the quiet as he runs fingers through long hair that spills over us.

I do not say anything, enjoying the touches on the skin that illuminates the walls and the surface of the water.

"I should return to the worksite. I've been gone too long already."

He was always going to return to the worker-peoples, though I had allowed me to forget. I enjoy the last few moments of skin touching.

"I'll come visit while we're here," he says.

"I will enjoy the visits," I say at length, not moving, not wanting to be released from this contented company.

He does not move either, and we linger a few moments longer, lounging on the smooth rock at the edge of the water.

When a clanging reverberates through the cave walls, I feel it in the rock beneath us, the air around us, the water around the feet, and in the being that is me. Croft stills a moment. He feels it, too. We both stand, and he looks at me with concern.

"This is not normal," I say as I pull him by the hand to dive into the pool.

At the well, we swim upward until I sense the large mass plunging through the surface of the pool and dropping toward us. Tightening a grip on the big hand, I dissolve us both into the water as the rock plummets through us to land with a thud at the bottom of the vertical shaft, then rolls down along the angled tunnel that stretches to the unknown.

I sweep the matter that is Croft with the matter that is me to disappear, reappearing at the cave entrance of the cliff face. He staggers a bit when we reform on the ledge.

A small scurry of peoples with heavy metal axpikes stands on the cliff. One people stands above the well, holding the pricklerod between spread legs and draining himself in an impressively long stream into the center of the well below. Another people swings an axpike to break another overhanging chunk off the rock face. Some peoples cheer as it tumbles into the well with a plunking splash.

These are not pilgrims come to celebrate. They are not mushrooms clinging to a shady log seeking to thrive. Nor are they beavers building protective shelter. This is blight without purpose or benefit. Destruction without cause or need.

A rare rage fires up within me and anger roils up in the belly. The white fluffs of clouds overhead gather and pile into a roiling gray mass above, and the water in the well effervesces wildly long after the ripples left by the fallen rock have dissipated.

These peoples will go down. After the rocks. And they will not resurface.

"I will remove them," I say, raising winds that kick up loose dirt and pelt the faces and skin of the blight-peoples.

"Wait," Croft says, wrapping an arm around me to pull me back into the shadows. "I'll take care of it. They're my responsibility."

I temper the anger, noting the frenzied energy roiling off him and joining with the energy around me. He can command the peoples; otherwise, I will cleanse the forest of this malignancy.

Clad in damp, clinging unders, Croft emerges from the obscured path to stalk onto the cliff. The expression he shows me is one I have only ever seen on the faces of peoples—murder. But the expression transforms into something more papa-like when he appears to them.

"Chief, you're here," one people says, holding a hand in the air to shield delicate skin from the flying debris.

"What is going on here?" Croft stands as bold as an eagle, chest proud and legs firmly braced.

At the look of the blight-peoples with iron tools backing down from Croft clad in wet, clinging braies, an unfamiliar sense of pride mixes with the blustering energy surrounding me.

"This rock. We thought we could use it for building."

"Stop," Croft orders. "Not this rock. It is the source of our water. This is where we celebrate Spring Rains." Croft says this in a tone that is level, not angry. The peoples grumble, but they listen to him.

"Take a break from work," he says. "Swim. Refresh yourselves then return to work. Downriver. Not here."

He retrieves the bundle of clothes from where it is tucked in the rocks. Some peoples climb down, while others strip down to unders.

A people, the one who broke a chunk of the cliff, remains standing, looking down into the well and gripping tight the handle of the axpike. I know the temptation of dropping things into the well. The bottom of the bend is littered with the histories of First Rains pilgrimages.

I am happy to oblige the curiosity that plays there in the dissatisfied eyes, the energy raging inside me not yet calmed.

I draw up a gust of wind and nudge him, but the heavy people stands firm. So I heave a bigger swell of energy at him, and I watch, unseen, as he tumbles over the edge of the cliff, iron axpike in hand. He breaks the surface of the water gracelessly and plummets like a rock.

If a people disappears in the well, they become food. That is the way of it. Energy.

Croft turns at the sound of the yelp that escaped the felled people before he went under. Exasperated shoulders slumping, he releases a heavy breath when he registers the hap. He casts a peeved look to the spot where I loom, unseen, but without pausing to think, he dives off the cliff into the well.

I follow on a breeze and relocate beneath the fallen axpike man to suspend him in the water—to aid Croft—until he can retrieve him. When Croft reaches the stunned worker-people, he removes the axpike still clutched in a tight fist. Then he pulls it and the people to the surface. I upsurge the water to give him a boost and push them out with haste.

By the time they surface, the other peoples have scurried at the edge of the pool to haul the man out. The rescued people sputters water, but he will endure. The peoples clap Croft on the back, celebrating the brave chief. Another wave of pride ripples through me.

When the scurry moves off to tend to the people who did not drown today, Croft turns on me. "What did you do?" he asks in a voice as cold as the deepest well waters.

"I was seeking balance. For the people to join the rocks he tumbled below."

"He could have died."

"Death is just a shifting of energies." *We spoke of this.* "Like diverting waters."

Big brown eyes grow wider than those of an owl before me, but they lack the mischief I am accustomed to.

"There are many bones at the bottom of the well." *It would not be so unusual,* I do not say.

"You would just take a life like that?"

Lives are not for me to take or give. I simply move energy. I do not voice this. He did not hear me before, and he will not hear me now with the energy vibrating off him like a disturbed wasp nest.

Mouth gaping open, he sputters. "Ah, ah... All those bones in the well?" he finally asks.

"Energy in flux," I say simply.

He looks at me with an expression that is stark, like land without water. The energy flowing off him vibrates with an unsettling ringing that gnaws on the sinew of being. *Fear?*

"I need to get my people back to camp," he says after a long moment of looking everywhere but at me.

I nod and dissipate into the boskage to watch as he and the peoples dress and gather tools. I watch from the rocky ledge as they return downstream, clapping each other on the back and cheering to the good fortune of the worker-people that was saved and to the bravery of Croft.

He will return later. He will hear me when the energy is calm like a turtle.

I float in the well, watching the sun set. The ripening clouds that signal the coming of First Rains gather in the sky.

Croft does not return, and for the first time in an eternal memory, I count time by the passing of the sun. When night comes, I evaporate and drift to the cliff to count stars.

He does not return the next day either, so I pad downstream. The river rocks press into the souls of the feet of this form, and cool water eddies around the knees and ankles. I reappear where the creek diverges to the dry bed to arrive at camp, unseen.

I shift energy to the heights of a tree and perch beside a nest of newly hatched beasties. The squawking of the anxious mama eases in the presence of the energy that is me, and she flies away without fear to find food for the chicklings.

The clouds gather as Croft moves among the worker-peoples. I feel when he senses me. The broad shoulders stiffen, and he stands upright. The words he speaks halt mid-command, but he recovers and resumes the work after a beat. The profile is intent; he does not look to where he senses me.

Curious.

When he walks away from the scurry of people to survey a dry well, I push a gentle pulse of energy to the back of him. Though the shoulders stiffen again, he does not look away from the hole. He does not look at me. But I sense him feeling me. The energy resonating in the air around us hums, but the back turned to me is a dam that diverts the flow between us. He is shielding himself like beavers that build high waters to protect lodge homes.

From me?

The energy in the air whirlpools around me. I am cold, but I draw on the surrounding heat and absorb it to swirl inside me. Hotter and faster, it churns, feeding a storm growing in the center of me.

The heart of me?

An unfamiliar confusion rails through me as the eddying of energy in the center of me tightens. It stutters a moment when I look to Croft, but the twisting inside me relents, growing into an erratic, fragmented pulsing force. I glance to the skies at the clouds, gathering faster and piling taller. *What is this chaotic cramping of waves, pounding at the air around me? Inside me?*

I no longer sense the traces of energy coming from him. They are disappeared in the chaos around me. Like a ghost.

A charge builds inside me, hot, angry friction, like the air before a dry thunderstorm. I blow out a breath to dispel the tightening energy. With the release, the clouds above let go an icy deluge. I do not look back at Croft or the peoples scampering for cover as I touch the ground.

I pad back to the well. I do not sense him behind me.

Several days pass. The worker-peoples finish the digging at the head of the dry creek bed and move to the next stretch of creek downriver. The clang-clanging in the ground grows dimmer as the quaduct progresses toward the towns.

The pilgrims come to celebrate First Rains, and from the depths of the well, I savor the joyful cheers of families laughing and brave ones plunging from the cliff. The delight and wonder that ripples through the air and water is a soothing presence.

Croft does not join them.

Four: Whispering Waters

The dry season is longer and dryer than cycles past, but the air is pregnant with moisture this day. The well has water, but the creek it feeds is dry, and the brush along the creek is brown.

All make do as the energies shift over the cycle flows. The beasties build homes closer to me or sleep through the dryer seasons. The boskage drives roots deeper or stores water within thickening flesh. First Rains are coming, though they are late this cycle.

I am drifting among the ripples on the surface of the pool, absorbing the heat of the sun, when a rhythmic clung-clung, clung-clung ripples in the water that flows through me. Drawing focus to the edges of the pool, I feel it again. Clung-clung, clung-clung.

It has been many cycles since peoples last came to check the quaduct downstream. They used to come each cycle before the First Rains, but the intervals between visits are greater and greater. In the wetter cycles, they come to clear the boskage from the quaduct. In dryer cycles, they come to line the quaduct beds and wells with clay that hardens in the sun.

When they come, I meander downstream, peering in the holes, listening to them argue over numbers, looking for a familiar face. A familiar face that never appears.

Clung-clung, clung-clung. The energy of the rhythmic clanging reverberates through me again. I dissolve into the water and emerge as vapor at the edge of the pool.

The clung-clung in the rocks below becomes a clomp-clomp, clomp-clomp in the air above. The steady rhythm bounces off the dry bed and the cliff face. I catch the wind to investigate the percussive echo.

Then a voice glides on the air in a whisper. "Silly Wehkya."

A memory?

A big beastie clomp-clomps toward me with a people riding her. He wears a brimmed hat, the hair beneath it silver and tied back in a tail. He wears gloves and leather pants, and a casual natural-colored tunic. With head turned to the dry bed, I think it must be more peoples coming to check the quaduct. For long moments, I watch, unseen, as the people rides at a steady trot until they reach the well. Despite the reverberation of heavy clomps, there is a familiar energy. Familiar, but different.

When the rider dismounts, I see a little metal horse hanging on a leather cord around the neck, and the face of the boy he once was. Croft is still striking, and though silver-haired and loose-skinned, he stands tall and proud. Despite the cycles that have passed, the presence of him—the energy that surrounds him—is warm, but the hum he emits is no longer smooth. A jagged twinge rubs at the edges rather than resonates.

"Silly Wehkya," he calls again. The voice is a comforting baritone that rumbles on the air but more rasped with age.

He is looking for me.

I know he senses me when a mischievous smile spreads across wide lips.

He tugs off the tunic and works off the leather boots, then the pants. Bundling the clothes into a neat pile, he drops the hat on top. He is paler than when I last saw him, and there are spots on the hands. He is beautiful still.

A winsome expression crosses the face in the moment before he dives into the water from the side of the pool. He emerges in the center and lies back to float with arms spread. As the water ripples around him, he watches the clouds with a fond gaze. The mischievous grin he wears conjures images of a rebellious childhood, brave explorations, and knowing energy.

Soon, he swims to the edge of the pool with strokes that are strong, though slower and more leisurely than they once were. He climbs out and stands at the base of the cliff. He arches backward to scrutinize the tall wall. Then he tests a craggy step with a veiny foot and grips the wall to begin the climb. I stay beneath him for support, but he is cautious. He scales the rock with the same poise he always did, though now the pace is slow and mindful.

On the precipice, he stands the way I remember. Fearless. Instead of diving into the water, he lowers himself to the edge of the cliff and dangles both legs over the side.

Gazing over the creek and the canopy of trees before him, he says the name again. "Silly Wehkya." An invitation to join him, spoken as softly as if he was lying next to me.

Not long after, Croft stands and stalks to the path hidden between the canopy of trees and the cliff face. I follow him and wrap the air around him as he sidesteps along the ledge to the cave entrance. He pokes a head inside and pauses before stepping into the dark. Inside, I generate a soft light on the walls for him.

When he reaches the breach in the cavern ahead, he steps out onto the ledge that overlooks the inner pool. The gasp he releases echoes on the interior walls. The water here is low now, and the drop to the surface is almost as far as the dive from the cliff into the well outside. There is no clear way to climb back out, and there are no other visible exits from this chamber.

"Silly Wehkya," he says, the name echoing off the walls and the surface of the black pool.

There is no fear in the energy surrounding him, but the erratic hitch that radiates off him persists. I want to reveal myself, but the memory of the dam he built between us stirs the roiling winds in the center of me. I do not want to be seen. I exist here, content in solitude.

I follow as Croft returns the way he came, sidestepping along the ledge outside. He stands on the cliff and studies the water for several breaths before he jumps off the edge feetfirst. He plunges into the water with a big splash. Ever brave, though he is more cautious in the winter cycle of life.

In the water, he dives into the depths and suspends himself underneath, waiting. Formless, I stay with him, embracing him within the swells of the energy that is me. He remains a long time below the surface.

I sense him feeling the energetic waves around us. The erratic hum of the pulses he emits flow with the steady tide of me. Instead of looking for the shape of me in the crystal green pool, he closes big brown eyes and lets me support him. In time, the energy radiating off him attunes with the energy rippling off me. When our hums resonate together, he surrenders and rests with me in the water.

We float for a long time in the cool spring as the water, the rocks, and the earth thrum with us.

In the evening, he cares for the peaceful beastie that drinks at the edge of the water and retrieves a pack. Slinging it over a shoulder, he climbs back to the precipice, where I join him again. He makes a fire and cooks a meal for himself. He makes a plate for me and leaves it on the rock next to him. That makes me smile, being seen without being seen.

When the sun sets, he lets the fire die, and he gazes at the canopy of stars. The energy that radiates off him is contented. I lie next to him under the night sky and listen to the breathing until it becomes snoring, a ragged, nasal rumbling that echoes around us. I roll him onto the side, and he stops.

In the morning, he sits in silence among the sounds of the wind in dry leaves and the tittering of birds and other beasties. He takes time to enjoy a morning meal of bread and cheese before packing the camp.

At the edge of the well, he lowers himself to knees that tremble. On hands spread wide on the rock, he touches forehead to the limestone rock. He exhales long until the lungs are empty of air. I feel the flush of energy that flows from him into me, the land, the air, the water.

Gratitude radiates off him. Then he inhales to fill the big lungs with fresh, clean air and a little of the energy that is me. He hums with the energy flowing over us.

I receive the gift and vibrate with the ground, the rocks, and the air. Then I flood the well, releasing a surge of water from the depths to fill the creek. Delight radiates off him, and the sudden laughter startles the birds in the nearby trees. Wet from the water now flowing around him, he shares a mischievous smile with me before he goes to find the big beastie.

I keep him company as he rides along the creek.

The cycle of peoples is short, fleeting like the boskage and the beasties. They grow and shift and evolve with the constant flow of water, ever renewing. He may not witness many more abundant rains or see beyond this cycle, but he will renew with them cycle after cycle.

FIVE: RIPPLING CYCLES

I pad through the forest, treading on the cool, damp earth. The desperate peeps of a chickling at the base of a fat oak draw my notice. It has fallen out of the nest, and when it senses me, it calls to me, little beak open wide with fervent peeps. Ants cover the feathery peeper.

Wiping them away, I wait until I hear a cawing from a panicked mama. She cannot help if the babelet cannot fly.

"Alright, little one. Just this once."

I flick more scrambling ants off the downy feathers. Cupping the tiny fluff in one hand, I dissolve into a breeze. It is not for me to deprive the ants of a feast, but I cannot watch the beasties suffer. Climbing to a branch high above, I settle her into the nest.

"Do not be so reckless. You may not be so lucky next time."

I glance to the skies, and raising a hand, I become the wind. I coast into the air to summon the clouds. It is time for First Rains.

About the Authors

JESSICA BRAWNER

Jessica Brawner, a versatile author hailing from Southern California, delves into both non-fiction and fiction realms with finesse. Her expertise spans from topical books on improving social interactions and the business of speaking and performing at libraries, to crafting captivating urban fantasy and steampunk tales. She has a blend of traditional publishing and self-publishing experience and finds that she prefers the latter. She shares her creative journey with her husband, Steven L. Sears.

NIKKI FLYNN

Nikki Flynn is a multi-genre writer, director, audio engineer and casting director for Phantasmal Bard Studios, her own brand of fiction with coauthor, Edwin Dantes. Her first two novels via Solstice Publishing, *Wanting Fangs: A Modern Gothic Romance* and *Forgotten and Found* have now been released.

S.R. PARADIGM

S.R. Paradigm loves books and tea, usually in that order. She is passionate about language and writing, and her works (and works-in-progress) span genres—though most of her experience is in the corporate, non-fiction realm, where she has thrived as a technical writer, trainer, and program manager.

JOHNNY ROACH

Johnny Roach is the author of Naan of Your Business. He lives with his children in Marietta, Ga.

DREA TALLEY

Drea Talley is a Struggling Writer™ and Chaotic Good bard. The kind of bard that tells stories and sings, but doesn't play an instrument because she gave up on the piano, was never good at the flute, and the guitar hurt her fingers. Her debut novel, *Seer of the Strait*, released in 2024, with the sequel, *Lady of the Bridges*, coming in the fall of 2025. She likes tea, tiny cakes, and snark.

JULIET WILDE

Juliet Wilde is a writer, a linguist, a mom, a wife, a storyteller, and an adventurer. She lives in Austin, Texas, with her husband, her little one, and a 120 lb German shepherd that makes a terrible watchdog.

Coming soon from Periapt Press...

LADY OF THE BRIDGES

The kingdom of Adalar, once a marvel of architecture and trade, was a crumbling shadow of its former glory when Carys Arslan, third generation seer and newly crowned Lady of the Bridges, arrived with her people. Carys is overwhelmed and out of her depth in her new kingdom, scrambling for allies and doing her best to become the Lady that Adalar needs. However, repairing the docks and keeping her growing kingdom fed aren't the only problems Carys faces.

Potential allies require thoughtful negotiations—the inland territory Dayira has offered resources in exchange for a promise of future aid and Veli wishes to strengthen relations—while steadfast relations with Vasi continue. Unknown agents of the Southern Empire, a new ward with a wild and unpredictable gift, and a growing number of proposals for an alliance marriage pull Carys in different directions. Can she remain true to herself and still do what is best for her kingdom?